Annie O'Neil spent most of her childhood with her leg draped over the family rocking chair and a book in her hand. Novels, baking and writing too much teenage angst poetry ate up most of her youth. Now Annie splits her time between corralling her husband into helping her with their cows, baking, reading, barrel racing (not really!) and spending some very happy hours at her computer, writing.

Also by Annie O'Neil

Her Knight Under the Mistletoe
Reunited with Her Parisian Surgeon
One Night with Dr Nikolaides

Hope Children's Hospital collection

Their Newborn Baby Gift
by Alison Roberts
One Night, One Unexpected Miracle
by Caroline Anderson
The Army Doc's Christmas Angel
The Billionaire's Christmas Wish
by Tina Beckett

Discover more at millsandboon.co.uk.

THE ARMY DOC'S CHRISTMAS ANGEL

ANNIE O'NEIL

MILLS & BOON

First published in Great Britain 2018
by Mills & Boon, an imprint of HarperCollins*Publishers*
1 London Bridge Street, London, SE1 9GF

Large Print edition 2019

© 2018 Harlequin Books S.A.

Special thanks and acknowledgement are given to Annie O'Neil for her contribution to the Hope Children's Hospital series.

ISBN: 978-0-263-07824-4

MIX
Paper from
responsible sources
FSC **FSC** **C007454**
www.fsc.org

Printed and bound in Great Britain
by CPI Group (UK) Ltd, Croydon, CR0 4YY

This one goes out to the
service men and women in our lives.

The sacrifices they make
are unimaginable.

The things they see and the work
they do can often come at a high cost.

Family life, physical health, even, in
those awful cases, loss of life.

And they still go out there and I hope
stories like this one prove we all
think their bravery and strength
are extraordinary.

CHAPTER ONE

"YOU PLANNING ON wearing a track into the floor?"

Finn looked across at his boss, startled to see him in the hospital given the hour, then gave a nonchalant shrug. "Maybe. What's it to you?"

Theo barked a good-natured laugh. "I paid for that floor. I was hoping we could keep it intact for a few more years before your lunking huge feet are embedded in it."

Finn looked down at the honey-colored floorboards then up at his boss as he scrubbed his hand through the tangles of his dark hair. About time he got a haircut. Or invested in a comb. It had only been…oh…about fourteen years since he'd given up the buzz cuts. Didn't stop him from thinking of himself as that fit, adrenaline-charged young man who'd stepped off the plane in Afghanistan all those years ago. Once an army man…

He took a step forward. The heat from his knee seared straight up his leg to his hip. An excruciating reminder that he was most definitely *not* an army man. Not ever again.

He gave Theo a sidelong look. "What are you doing here, anyway? It's late."

"Not that late." Theo looked at his watch as if that confirmed it was still reasonable to be treading the hospital boards after most folk were at home having their tea. "I could ask you the same question."

It was Avoidance Technique for Beginners and both men knew it.

They stared at one another, without animosity but unwilling to be the first to break. Lone wolf to lone wolf…each laying claim to the silence as if it were an invisible shield of strength.

Heaven knew why. It was hardly a secret that Finn was treating one of the hospital's charity patients who was winging in from Africa today. He just…he was grateful to have a bit of quiet time before the boy arrived. His leg pain was off the charts today and once Adao arrived, he'd like to be in a place where he could assure the kid that life without a limb was worth living.

"Want to talk about it?" Theo looked about as excited to sit down and have a natter about feelings as Finn did.

"Ha! Good one." Finn flicked his thumb toward the staff kitchen tucked behind the floor's reception area. "I'll just run and fill up the kettle while you cast on for a new Christmas jumper, shall I?"

Theo smirked then quickly sobered. "I'm just saying, if you ever want to…" he made little talky mouths with his hands "…you know, I'm here."

"Thanks, mate." He hoped he sounded grateful. He was. Not that he'd ever take Theo up on the offer.

It wasn't just trusting Theo that was the issue. It was trusting himself. And he wasn't there yet. Not by a long shot. Days like today were reminders why he'd chosen to live a solitary existence. You got close to people. You disappointed them. And he was done disappointing people.

Christmas seemed to suck the cheer—what little he had—right out of him. All those reminders of family and friendship and "togetherness." Whatever the hell that was.

He didn't do any of those things. Not anymore.

All the jolly ward decorations, staffrooms already bursting with mince pies, and festive holiday lights glittering across the whole of Cambridge didn't seem to make a jot of difference.

He scanned the view offered by the floor-to-ceiling windows and rolled his eyes.

He was living in a ruddy 3D Christmas card and wasn't feeling the slightest tingle of hope and anticipation the holiday season seemed to infuse in everyone else.

Little wonder considering…

Considering nothing.

He had a job. He had to do it. And having his boss appear when he was trying to clear his head before Adao arrived wasn't helping.

He'd been hoping to walk the pain off. Sometimes it worked. Sometimes, like today, it escalated the physical and, whether he cared to admit it or not, emotional reminders of the day his life had changed forever.

Should've gone up to the rooftop helipad instead. No one ever really went there in the winter. Although this year the bookies were tipping the scales in favor of snow. Then it really would be like living in a Christmas card.

"Why are you here? Was there some memo about an all-staff welcoming committee?" Finn knew there wasn't. He was just giving his boss an out if he wanted it. Bloke talk came in handy for a lot of emotional bullet dodging.

Theo sighed. "Ivy."

Finn lifted his chin in acknowledgement. Her mystery illness had been the talk of all the doctors' lounges. "Gotta be tough, mate."

"'Tis." Theo flicked his eyes to the heavens, gave his stippled jaw a scrub and gave an exasperated sigh. "I hate seeing her go through this. She's five years old. You know?"

Oh, yeah. He knew. It was why he'd retrained as a pediatric surgeon after the IED had gone off during a standard patrol. The loss of life that day had been shameful.

All of them children.

Who on this planet targeted *children*?

At least he'd had an enemy to rail against. Theo was shooting in the dark at a mystery illness. No wonder the guy had rings under his eyes.

"Had anything good today?" Topic-changing was his specialty.

Theo nodded. "A few interesting cases actually." He rattled through a few of them. "Enough to keep me distracted."

Finn huffed out an "I hear you" laugh. Work was the only way he kept his mind off the mess he'd made of his personal life.

You're on your own now, mate. Paying your penance, day by day.

"The diagnostician. She managed to clear her schedule yet?"

Theo nodded. "Took a bit of juggling but she's here now."

Finn waited for some more information—something to say what Theo thought of her—but received pure silence. Any topic related to Ivy was a highly charged one so it looked like his boss was going to reserve judgment on the highly touted globetrotter until she'd had a bit more time with his daughter.

"What's her name again?" Finn tried again when Theo obviously wasn't going to comment further. "I heard one of the nurse's call her Godzilla."

Theo gave a sharp tsk.

He didn't like gossip. Or anything that stood in the way of the staff acting as a team. "She's a bit of a loner. Might give off a cooler edge than some of the staff are used to. Particularly around the holidays. But she's not yet had a chance to get her feet on the ground, let alone establish a rapport with the entire staff." He gave Finn a quick curt nod, making it very clear that he let facts stand. Not rumor. "She's called Madison Archer. Doesn't get much more American than that, does it?"

"Short of being scented like apple pie, I guess not." Finn smiled at Theo, trying to add a bit of levity, but raised his hands in apology at Theo's swiftly narrowed eyes.

More proof, as if he needed it, that Finn was no star at chitchat. He called a spade a spade, and other than that his conversational skills were operating on low to subterranean.

Theo's expression shifted to something indecipherable. "It's at times like this I understand how the parents feel when they walk in the doors of our hospital. Makes it that much more important we treat each other with respect. Without that, how can we respect our patients? Ourselves?" He lifted up his hands as if seeking an answer from the universe then let them fall with a slap against his long legs.

They looked at one another a moment in silence. This time with that very same respect he'd just spoken of.

Theo was a class-A physician and this hospital—the hospital he'd *built*—was one of the finest in the world, and still not one of them could put a finger on what was behind Ivy's degenerating condition. Lethargy had become leg pain. Leg pain had escalated to difficulty walking. They were even considering admitting her full time, instead of dipping in and out, things were so bad.

How the hell Theo went about running the hospital day in, day out when his little girl was sick...it would've done his head in.

Precisely why being on his own suited Finn to a T. No one to worry about except his patients. No emotions holding him back...as long as he kept his thoughts on the future and his damn leg on the up and up.

He gave his head a sharp shake, silently willing Theo to move on. A wince of pain narrowed the furrows fanning out from his eyes as he shifted his weight fully onto his right leg.

The infinitesimal flick of Theo's eyes down then back up to Finn's face meant the boss man knew precisely what was going on. But he knew better than to ask. Over a decade of wearing the prosthetic leg and he still hadn't developed a good relationship with the thing. The number of times he'd wanted to rip it from his knee and hurl the blasted contraption off the roof...

And then where would he be? In a wheelchair like Ivy?

Nah. That wasn't for him.

Helping children just like her—and Adao, who'd learned too much about war far too soon—were precisely why he kept it on. Standing beside the operating table was his passion. And if that meant sucking up the building pressure and tolerating the sharp needles of pain on occasion? Then so be it.

"Well..." He tried to find something positive to say and came up with nothing so fell back on what he knew best. Silence.

After a few minutes of staring out into the

inky darkness he asked Theo, "You heard anything about the boy's arrival time?"

Finn was chief surgeon on the case, but Theo had a way of knowing just that little bit more than his staff. Sign of a good leader if ever there was one.

"Adao?"

Finn nodded, unsurprised that out of a hospital full of children Theo knew exactly who he was referring to. Although they didn't have too many children flying in from Africa just a handful of weeks before Christmas.

Then again, war never took much time to consider the holidays.

"Did they get out of the local airport in Kambela all right?" Theo asked.

"Yeah." Finn had received an email from one of the charity workers who'd stayed behind at the war-torn country's small clinic. "Touch and go as to whether the ceasefire would hold, but they got off without a hitch. They say his condition's been stabilized, but the risk of infection—" He stopped himself. Infection meant more of the arm would have to come off. Maybe the shoulder. Flickers of rage crackled through him like electricity.

This was a kid. A little *kid*. As if growing up in a country ravaged by war wasn't bad enough.

There had been a fragile negotiated peace in the West African country for a few months now, but thousands of landmines remained. The poor kid had been caught in a blast when another little boy had stepped on one. That boy had died instantly. The second—Adao—suffice it to say his life would never be the same.

They'd been out playing. Celebrating another renewal of the ceasefire. The horror of it all didn't bear thinking about.

Not until he saw the injuries, assessed damage limitation, talked Adao through how he would always feel that missing arm of his, but—

Don't go there, man. You *made it. The kid'll make it.*

Hopefully he wouldn't actively push his family away the way Finn had. If he had any leanings toward giving advice, he'd put that top of the list.

Keep those you love close to you.

Pushing them away only made the aching hole of grief that much harder to fill.

He knew that now.

Theo pulled his phone out of his pocket and thumbed through the messages. "He was meant to have been choppered in from London a couple of hours ago, right? The charity texted a while back saying something about paperwork and customs, but you'd think a boy with catastrophic injuries would outweigh a bit of petty bureaucracy."

Finn brought his fist down on a nearby table. That sort of hold-up was unacceptable. Especially with a child's welfare at stake.

"Hey!" Theo nodded at the table, brow creased. "You'd better apologize."

"What?" Disbelief flashed across Finn's features then a smile. "You want me to say sorry to the table? Sorry, table. I don't know what got into me." He held his hands out wide. *Happy now?* the gesture read.

Theo closed the handful of meters between them with a few long-legged strides, crossed his arms over his chest and looked Finn square in the eyes. "Are you all right to handle this?"

His hospital. His terms.

Fair enough.

"'Course." Finn said. "But if you think I'm not up to it? Take me off. Bear in mind you'll have to drag me out of here and nurse the black eyes of whoever you think can operate on Adao better than me."

No point in saying he'd have to deliver the punches from a wheelchair if his knee carried on mimicking a welding iron.

He ground his back teeth together and waited. Theo knew as well as he did that the last thing he'd do was punch someone. But it was Theo's hospital. Theo's call.

Theo feigned giving Finn a quick one-two set of boxing punches, making contact with his midsection as he did.

Finn didn't budge. He had a slight edge on Theo in height, weight and age. The Grand Poo-bah of Limb Specialists, they'd once joked.

"Look at that." Finn's tone was as dry as the Sahara. "I'm turning the other cheek."

Theo widened the space between them and whistled. "Have you been working out again?"

Finn smiled. Always had. Always would.

Pushing himself to the physical limit was one of the things that kept the demons at bay.

Theo gave Finn's shoulder a solid clap. "You're the one I want on this. The only one." He didn't need to spell out to Finn how his time in the military had prepared him more than most for the injuries Adao had sustained. "Just want to make sure you're on top form when the little guy arrives."

"What? Nah." Finn waved away his concerns, gritting his teeth against the grinding of his knee against his prosthesis. "I just save this curmudgeon act for you. Someone's gotta be the grumpy old man around here."

"I thought that was Dr. Riley."

They both laughed. Dr. Riley had yet to be seen without an ear-to-ear grin on his face. The man had sunbeams and rainbows shooting out of his ears. The children adored him. Most people called him Dr Smiley.

Finn nodded toward the Christmas tree twinkling away in the dimly lit reception area where they stood. "A bit early, isn't it?"

"Not if you're Evie."

Finn grunted. Evie was the resident Mrs. Claus around Hope Children's Hospital. Especially now she was all loved up. Just being around her and Ryan made him...well... suffice it to say it brought up one too many memories he'd rather not confront. Love. Marriage. They'd never got as far as the baby carriage, he and Caroline. Now he supposed he never would.

Guess that made him the resident Scrooge. Not that he had anything against Christmas in particular, it was just…seeing these poor kids in hospital over the holidays always bugged him. He may not want to hang out with his own family, but he was damn sure these kids wanted nothing more than their mums and dads at the end of their beds on Christmas morning.

"Anyone else about for Adao's arrival?"

Finn shook his head. "Not that I know about. I've got the usual suspects lined up for tomorrow so we can give him a proper assessment." He listed a few names. "Right." He clapped his hands together. "I'm going to get on up to the roof, if you don't mind. Clear the cobwebs before Adao arrives." He stood his ground. Theo was smart enough to take the absence of movement as his cue to leave and turned toward the bank of elevators.

"Hey," Theo called over his shoulder as he was entering the elevator. "You know we have a team of experts who look after that sort of thing."

Theo didn't have to look at Finn's knee for Finn to know what he was talking about. He knew the offer was there. He just didn't want to take it. Pain equaled penance. And he had a helluva lot of making up to do. Parents. Brother. Ex-wife. Friends. And the list went on.

"Good to know." He waited until the elevator doors closed before he moved.

A string of silent expletives crossed his lips as he hobbled over to a sofa, pulled up his trouser leg and undid the straps to ease the ache in his knee, not even caring when the whole contraption clattered to the floor.

One breath in…one breath out…and a silent prayer of thanks that he had this moment alone. He didn't do weak.

Not in public anyway.

The handful of moments he'd let himself slide into self-pity over the years…those would remain buried in his chest as bitter reminders of the paths he shouldn't have taken. The lessons he should've learned.

He gave his prosthesis a bit of a kick.

"It's just you and me, mate. Guess we'd better start finding a way to make nice."

CHAPTER TWO

"ARE YOU HANGING about for a meet-and-greet with Adao?"

Naomi went wide-eyed at Evie's question. She hadn't said anything, but that had definitely been her plan. A volley of responses ricocheted round her chest and lodged in her throat because she didn't want Evie to hear any of them.

I know how he feels.

He's probably as scared as I was.

I wanted him to know there's someone here who understands what it's like to live in a world ruled by guns and fear.

But Evie knew nothing of Naomi's past. Having Adao here would be the biggest emotional challenge she'd faced since arriving in Britain at the ripe age of fifteen. Scared. Utterly alone.

Two things she never wanted Adao to feel.

At least he knew his family was waiting at home for him.

Naomi pinned on her bright smile—the one she ensured her patients and colleagues knew her by—and asked, "How'd you guess?"

Evie shrugged in her elfin way. She just did.

Naomi liked to think of Evie as the entire hospital's resident Christmas faerie. She had a canny knack for intuiting things. That and a heart the size of Britain. She smiled as Evie shifted Grace on her hip, the baby who'd been abandoned at the hospital a few months ago and who was to be adopted by Evie and her soon-to-be husband, Ryan.

"I have a really ridiculous question." Evie looked at her a bit bashfully.

"Shoot."

"I'm not exactly sure where Kambela is."

"Adao's home?" Naomi knew what Evie was really asking. *Is it anywhere near where you're from?* Her English, no matter how hard she tried, was still lightly accented. "It's on the coast of Africa. Near the Horn."

Right next door to her country. Zemara.

"Hey...is everything all right with you?"

Uh-oh. Evie's emotional intuition radar was beep-beep-beeping like a metal detector in her direction...not so good.

"Fine! Great." Naomi tipped her head toward the glass doors leading out of the front of the hospital and grinned. "Did you see that?"

"Violet being discharged early? Amazing. You did such good work with her." Evie grinned and shifted Grace from one arm to the other. "*Oof!* This little girl's putting on weight at a rate of knots! I'll have 'mom arms' soon."

Naomi smiled and gave the tip of the baby's nose a tickle. Hope Hospital had hit the headlines with this little girl and would again soon with Adao…if the surgery went well and the rehab was successful. So much of recovery had to do with a patient's will. The will to fight. The desire to survive. The stamina to confront what had happened to them head on.

She crossed her fingers behind her back for Adao, ignoring the tight twist of nerves constricting the oxygen in her lungs.

"Are you waiting for Ryan?"

Evie nodded, her smile hitting the ear-to-ear register. If a couple of red-breasted robins flew in the front door and began adorning her with mistletoe, she could easily be the poster girl for Cupid's arrow. "He's just come out of surgery. I'm swotting up for nursing college in the new term and he's promised to talk me through all the signs, symptoms and early treatment for scarlet fever if I make him an early Christmas dinner."

"Turkey and all the trimmings?" Naomi couldn't hide her shock. She knew they were in love, but Christmas dinner on a "school night"?

"Giant prawn cocktails and pavlova." Evie shrugged and shifted Grace in her arms again. Whatever her Australian-born fiancé wanted…

Naomi giggled. "You are well and truly loved up, aren't you?"

Evie blushed in response. Her whole world had changed. "It's not just me, is it? Have you seen Alice lately? Sunbeams. Everywhere she goes. And Marco can't stop humming opera during surgery these days." She drummed her free fingers on her chin and gave Naomi a mischievous sideways look. "I wonder who's next?"

Naomi put up her hands and laughed. "Not me!" That ship of possibility had sailed long ago.

"Why not? You're beautiful. Amazing at your job. You'd be a real catch."

If cowardice was something a man could ever love, sure. But it wasn't. Which was precisely why she kept herself just out of love's reach.

She was just about say "Finn Morgan" to be contrary, but stopped herself. The man had scowling down to a fine art. At least around her. But the season of good cheer was upon them so she stuck to what had served her best when her past pounded at that locked door at the back of her mind: a positive attitude. "I reckon Mr. Holkham down in the cafeteria could do with a bit of a love buzz."

Evie threw back her head and laughed. "A love buzz? I don't know if that's a bit too energetic for him. What is he? Around seventy?"

"I think so. I love that Theo hired retirees who wanted to keep active, but…if anyone needs a love buzz it's him." She made a silly face. "Anything to make him chirpier when he serves up the lasagna. Who wants garlic bread with a side of gloom?"

"Good point."

Naomi could almost see the wheels turning in Evie's mind…already trying to figure out who she could couple with the sweet, if not relatively forlorn, older gentleman. She'd tried to tease a smile from him every day since the hospital had opened, to no avail. Perhaps she should ask him for a coffee one day. Maybe he was just lonely. A widower.

She knew more than most that with love came loss and that's why being cheerful, efficient and professional was her chosen modus operandi.

"Ooh, Gracie, look. It's Daddy!" Evie took her daughter's teensy hand and made it do a little wave as Ryan approached with a broad smile and open arms.

Naomi gave Evie's arm a quick squeeze and smiled. "I'd better get up there."

"All right. I'll leave you to it, then," Evie said distractedly, her eyes firmly fixed on her future husband.

Naomi took the stairs two at a time all the way up to the fifth floor, as she usually did. She put on the "feel good" blinkers and refocused her thoughts. She was feeling genuinely buoyed by her last session. A cheer-worthy set of results for her patient followed by a discharge. What a way to end a work day!

Watching a little girl skip—*skip!*—hand in

hand with her parents straight out of the hospital doors and away home, where she would be able to spend Christmas with her family. A Christmas miracle for sure. Four months ago, when Violet had been helicoptered in from a near-fatal car accident, Naomi had had her doubts.

It was on days like this her job was the perfect salve to her past. Little girl power at its finest. And knowing she was playing a role in it made it that much better.

If she could keep her thoughts trained on the future, she could hopefully harness some of that same drive and determination in Adao. This was definitely not the time to let her own fears and insecurities bubble to the surface.

Then again, when was it the time?

Never. That was when.

So! Eyes on the prize and all would be well.

She hit the landing for the fifth floor and did a little twirl before pushing the door open.

Happy, happy, happy— *Oh.*

Not so happy.

The doctor's hunched shoulders and pained expression spoke volumes.

And not just any doctor.

Finn Morgan.

Of all the doctors at Hope, he was the one she had yet to exchange a genuine smile with. Well…him and the cafeteria chap, but she had to work with Mr. Morgan and he made her feel edgy. The man didn't do cheery. Not with her anyway.

Some days she had half a mind to tell him to snap out of it. He was a top surgeon at an elite private hospital. He worked on cases only the most talented of surgeons could approach with any hope of success. And still… King of the Grumps.

It wasn't as if he wasn't surrounded by people doing their best to create a warm, loving environment at Hope Hospital, no matter what was going on in their personal lives.

Not that she'd ever admit it, but most days she woke up in a cold sweat, her heart racing and arms reaching out for a family she would never see again.

If she could endure that and show up to work with a smile on her face, then whatever was eating away at him could be left at home as well.

She pushed the door open wider, took a step

forward then froze. Her breath caught in her throat at the sound of the low moan coming from his direction. As silently as she could, she let the door from the stairwell close in front of her so that all she could see of him through the small glass window was his rounded back moving back and forth as he kneaded at something. His knee? His foot? She'd noticed a slight limp just the once but the look he'd shot her when he'd realized she'd seen it had been enough to send her scuttling off in the other direction.

Even so...

He was sitting all alone in the top floor's central reception area, his back to her, the twinkling lights of the city beyond him outlining his broad-shouldered physique.

Her gut instinct was to go to Finn... *Mr. Morgan*, she silently corrected herself...but the powerful "back off" vibes emanating from him kept her frozen at the stairwell door.

She'd been flying so high after finishing with Violet she'd thought she'd put her extra energy to use helping Adao settle in. She'd already been assigned as his physiotherapist—work that wouldn't begin until after his surgery with

Finn Morgan—but she thought meeting him today might help him know there was someone who understood his world. His fears.

She pressed her hand against the glass as another low moan traveled across from the sofa where Finn remained resolutely hunched over his leg.

Something about his body language pierced straight through to her heart. A fellow lost soul trying to navigate a complicated world the best he could?

Or just a grump?

From what she'd seen, the man wouldn't know a good mood if it bit him on the nose.

She pulled her gaze away from him and searched the skyline for Adao's helicopter. She'd come here to find her patient, not snoop on a doctor clearly having a private moment.

She had little doubt the little boy was experiencing so many things that she had all those years ago when she'd arrived in the UK from Zemara. The language barrier. The strange faces. No family.

She swallowed against the lump forming in her throat and squeezed her eyes tight.

It was a long time ago.

Eleven years, two months and a day, to be exact.

Long enough to have moved on.

At least that's what logic told her. But how did you ever forget the day you saw everyone you loved herded into a truck and driven away off to the mountains? Mountains rumored to be scarred with pre-dug mass graves for anyone the rebels deemed unfit for their indiscriminatingly cruel army.

Blinking back the inevitable sting of tears, she gave herself a sharp shake and forced herself to paste on a smile. Her life was a good one. She was doing her dream job. In one of the most beautiful cities in the world, no less. Every day she was able to help and nurture children who, against the odds, always found a way to see the good in things.

So that's what she did, too. Focusing on the future was the only way she had survived those early days. And the only way she could live with herself now.

She pressed her forehead to the small, cool window in the door. In the dimly lit reception area—the lights were always lowered after seven at night—Finn had turned his face so that she could clearly see his profile.

He was a handsome man. Not storybook English—blond and blue-eyed, the way she'd once imagined everyone looked before she'd arrived in the UK. More…rugged, as if he'd just stepped off a plane from a long, arduous trek across the Alps rather than a doctor who had taken the elevator up from the surgical ward where he could usually be found. Not that she'd been stalking him or anything. Far from it. He was an arm's-length kind of guy judging by the handful of terse encounters they'd had.

Come to think of it, every time their paths had crossed since the hospital had opened— either going into or coming out of a session— he'd bristled.

Physically bristled.

Not the usual effect she had on people but, hey…she didn't need to be his bestie, she just needed a quality working relationship. That… and a bit of professional respect would be nice. Having seen his work on a near enough daily basis, she knew he respected her work…it would just be nice if that respect included the occasional smile or "Thank you."

His hair was a rich, dark brown. A tangled mess of waves that could easily turn to curls if it grew out. He was a big man. Not fat. No. Tall and solidly built. A "proper" man, as her birth mother would have said. A real man.

She swallowed back the sting of tears that inevitably followed when she thought of her mother. Her beautiful mother, who had worked so hard to pay for her extra lessons from any of the aid workers who had been based out of her hometown for as long as she could remember.

And then, of course, there was also her foster mother. The one who had taught her that she still had it in her to be brave. Face the maze of applications she needed to complete to get into medical school one day and, eventually, fulfil her dream of working as a pediatric physiotherapist.

Touch, she'd come to realize, was one of the most curative things of all.

Finn shifted around on the sofa and— Oh!

Her fingers wove together and she pressed her hands to her mouth to stem her own cry. He wore a prosthesis. She'd had no idea.

And from the looks of things, his leg was hurting. A man as strong and capably built as

Finn would have to be in some serious pain to look the way he did now. Slightly ashen. Breath catching. Unaware of everything else around him.

Instinct took over.

Before she thought better of it, she was by his side.

"Please. Perhaps I can help massage..." The rest of her offer died on her lips as she saw equal hits of horror and anger flash across his gray eyes.

She stood, completely frozen, mesmerized by their near-mystical depths.

How had she never noticed them before? So...haunted. She wondered if her dark eyes looked the same.

"What are you doing here?" Finn hastily grabbed his prosthesis and strapped it back on, despite the redness she saw engulfing his knee.

"I was just— I..."

I wanted to help.

"Well?" Finn rose alongside her, the scent of cotton and forest hitting her senses as he did.

She was tall so it took a lot of height to make her feel small. If the irritation radiating from him wasn't making her feel as if she'd invaded an incredibly private moment, she could almost imagine herself feeling delicate in his presence.

Delicate?

What was that about?

Finn scanned her uniform for her employee badge, though she was sure he already knew her name. It was his signature on the forms requesting her as Adao's physio.

She sucked in a breath. This was about Adao, not about Finn. Although...

Not your business. You have your secrets. He has his.

"Sorry. Please. I didn't mean to interrupt."

"No." Finn stared at her for a moment then swiped at the air between them, causing her to flinch. "What do you need?"

"I-I was here to help with Adao," she stammered. "I thought perhaps I could help settle him in."

"What?" Finn bridled. "You think I'm not up to being my patient's welcoming committee?"

She tilted her head to the side and pinched her lower lip with her teeth. Was he hoping for an honest answer? Or was this the famous British sense of humor at play?

Her silence seemed to give him the "No" he was expecting. His swift change of expression told her he was already dismissing her.

So much for trying to go the extra mile! She was about to tell him Adao was her patient too when, mercifully, Finn's phone buzzed and those penetrating, moonstone-colored eyes of his relaxed their spotlight grip on her.

He was as chatty on the phone as he was with her. A few responses of "Yeah. Yeah. Got it…" later and he was beckoning her to join him.

Okay.

He swiftly crossed to the bank of elevators—so quickly it was difficult to see how he hid the pain—and punched the illuminated button as he pulled his key card out of his pocket. Only staff were allowed up onto the roof and the magnetic key cards were the only way of taking the elevator up there. "Adao's ten minutes out. You done any helicopter arrivals before?"

She shook her head. Not here anyway. She'd seen more than her fair share before she'd left Zemara, but usually those helicopters had been filled with rebels wielding machine guns. Not charity workers with patients about to undergo life-altering surgery.

"Right." Finn pulled a crumpled bit of note-paper out of his pocket. "Adao's seven years old, suffering from—"

"Multiple injuries as a result of a land-mine explosion," Naomi cut in. She'd read the case. Memorized it. It had all but scored itself straight into her heart if the truth be told, but that wasn't what this showdown was about. She kept on talking as the elevator doors opened and the hit of wintry air all but took her breath away. "Adao's injuries include loss of his right arm. Efforts have been made to keep infection to a minimum, but our goal is to ensure he retains as much use of his shoulder as possible so that any use of a pros—' She stopped, her eyes clashing with Finn's—*Mr. Morgan's*—as he wheeled on her.

"Fine. Good. I see you're up on the case. How's about we have a bit of quiet time before the chaos begins, yeah?"

Naomi nodded and looked away, forcing herself to focus on the crisp, starlit sky above them.

No problem.

She'd obviously seen far more than Finn— *Mr. Morgan*—had wanted her to. An incredibly private moment for a man who clearly didn't do vulnerability.

Vulnerability and strength were two of the reasons she'd chosen to work at Hope. Most of the children here were going through something frightening. Loss of a limb. Surgery. Illnesses that meant they would be facing a future that would present hurdle after hurdle. And despite all the pain and all the suffering, the bulk of the children confronted their futures with a courage that amazed her on a daily basis. If she could be a part of making their future something to actually look forward to, then she was going to give it her all.

She tipped her head up and let the wind skid across her features as she sought out the Milky Way. The night was so clear she spotted it almost instantly. She was constantly amazed by the band of light made up of so many stars, so faraway, they were indistinguishable to the naked eye. In Zemara, they called the spiral galaxy they were such a small part of the Path of Spirits. This was where her family must be now...far above her...looking down...

A rippling of goose-pimples shot across her arms, but it wasn't the cold that had instigated them.

Guilt had a lot to answer for. Here she was at one end of the galaxy while her family were... only heaven knew where. It wasn't fair.

"Look." Finn's rich voice broke through the thick silence. "Over there."

She turned and followed the line of his arm and saw the helicopter emerging from the darkness.

CHAPTER THREE

NAOMI'S EYES WERE trained on the helicopter but all Finn could focus on was her.

Why had he snapped at her like he had?

It wasn't her fault she'd seen him in the lounge…without his leg…exposed as the embittered man he'd become ever since the future he'd thought he'd have had literally been torn away from him.

It also wasn't her fault that every time he saw her his senses shot to high alert. There was no way he was going to put a name to what he felt each time their paths crossed, but his body was miles ahead of him on that front.

A white-hot, solitary flame had lit that very first staff meeting when they'd all gathered together in the hospital's huge atrium and he'd first seen her. Even at—what had she been? Fifty meters from him? Twenty? Whatever. The impact had been sharp, forceful, and, if today was anything to go by, unabating.

From the response his body had had to her, she may as well have sashayed up to him in a curve-hugging negligee and wrapped him round one of her long, elegant fingers.

Not that he'd thought about her naked.

Okay, fine. Of course he had.

But it had just been the once, and the woman had all but floated out of the hospital's therapy pool in a scarlet swimsuit that had made him jealous of the droplets of water cascading down her body.

What else was he meant to do?

Treat her with respect, you numpty.

Everything about her commanded a civility he could tap into for the rest of his colleagues, but Naomi? Whatever it was he felt around her it meant he simply wasn't able to extend it to her. Not in the manners department anyway.

Naomi's entire essence sang of grace and an innate sensitivity to both her patients and her environment. Her movements were always smooth. Fluid. Her voice was carefully modulated, lightly accented, but he didn't know from where. He'd thought of asking once or twice, but that would've verged on curious and with half the hospital staff staggering around the hospital with love arrows embedded in their hearts…bah. Whatever. He should just stuff his hormones in the bin and have done with them.

And yet…even now, with her head tipped back as it was, the wind shifting along that exquisitely long neck of hers, there was something almost regal about Naomi's presence. Not haughty or standoffish, more…wise.

Where he shot from the hip, she always took a moment before responding to his sharp comments and brusque reactions to her.

She wasn't to know his brush-offs were the age-old battle of desire versus pragmatism.

Where he felt big and lunky, she was lithe and adroit.

Long-limbed. Sure-footed. High, proud cheekbones. Skin the shade of… He didn't know to describe it. A rich, warmly colored brown? Whatever shade it was, it was beautiful. The perfect complement to her full, plump mouth. Not that he was staring at it. Much.

There was something fiercely loyal shining in those dark eyes of hers. He saw it whenever she was with a patient. But he could also see it now as she trained her eyes on the sky above. For whom or what it shone, he would never know, because he didn't do personal. Didn't do intimate. Not anymore.

As if feeling his gaze on her, she turned and met his eyes.

"Is there anywhere we're meant to stand when they land, Mr. Morgan?"

Finn scowled. Why'd she have to catch him mooning over her? And what was with this *Mr. Morgan* business? Made him sound like a grumpy old man.

Humph.

Maybe that was the point she was making.

"It's Finn," he said. "Over there." He pointed toward the covered doorway where a porter was wheeling a gurney into place then turned his focus on to the approaching helicopter… willing the beats and syncopation of the blades cutting through the thin, wintry air to knock some sense back into him.

Bah.

He hadn't been mooning. It had simply been a while. Once he'd cut ties with his past, he'd thought that part of him had all but died.

He should be relieved his body was still capable of responding to a woman like a red-blooded male. So many of the soldiers he'd met during his stint in hospital…hell…he didn't wish their futures on his worst enemies.

All these thoughts and the raft of others that inevitably followed in their wake fell to the wayside as the helicopter hovered above them for a moment before executing a perfect landing.

And then they all fell to what they did best, caring for their patient.

There were too many people in Adao's room. It was easy enough to see from the growing panic in his wide, dark eyes as they darted from person to medical contraption to yet another person.

When they landed on her, all she could see was fear.

He was strapped to the gurney, completely surrounded by medical staff from the charity and the hospital all exchanging stats and information at a rate of knots that would have been impossible for him to comprehend.

Short, sharp counts dictated the swift shift from the gurney to the hospital bed and yet another stream of instructions flowed over him as they hooked him up to fresh IVs and peeled out another ream of information as they pressed monitors to his skinny, bare, little-boy chest. And when he called out for his parents it was all she could do not to tear her heart from her own chest.

"It's too much!"

The room fell silent as all eyes turned to Naomi.

"I beg your pardon?"

Finn hadn't moved a muscle, but his voice may as well have been a drill boring straight into her chest for the pain it caused.

She lifted her chin and met his steel-colored gaze. Yes, she was still smarting from his curt form of issuing orders.

"Not on that side."

"Not too close."

"Not too far."

There didn't seem to be a single thing she could do properly under his hawk-eyed gaze. But when it came to the child—*this child*—enough was enough.

"Please. Give the boy some peace. He's known nothing but chaos. This place—this hospital—must bring him peace. Comfort. Not fear."

Finn's eyebrows lifted a notch. It was written all over his face. She'd overstepped the mark.

Just as she was about to run out of the room, find a computer and start composing her letter of resignation, he spoke.

"You heard Naomi." He pointed at one nurse and one doctor, both of whom were on the overnight shift in Adao's ward. "You two stay. The rest of you…" He made a shooing motion with his hands. "Out you go. And you…' He pointed directly at Naomi. "You come with me."

Finn's eyes were glued to Naomi's throat. The tiny pulse point, alive with a blaze of passion he'd not seen in her before.

Their paths had never really crossed in this way. Neither had their temperaments.

Fighting for a patient.

It showed her high-energy, positive approach to work was more than skin deep.

But what he wanted to get to was the *why*. Why this little boy? Why the specifics? Her slight accent intrigued him. Maybe it was from a French-speaking country? He wasn't sure. Either way, there was something about Adao that had got under her skin and was making an emotional impact.

Problem Number One.

Finn flexed his fingers, hoping it would rid them of the urge to reach out and touch her throat, smooth his thumb across her pounding pulse point. From the meter or so he'd put between them, he could still tell her skin looked as soft as silk. But her spirit? Solid steel.

The combination pounded a double hit onto his senses. Primal. Cerebral.

Problem Number Two.

He bashed the primal response into submission and channeled his thoughts into figuring out what made her tick.

Work.

That much was obvious. Not that he kept tabs on the woman, but he'd only ever seen her in work clothes. Never did she shift to casual or night-out-on-the-town outfits as loads of other doctors did when they threw their scrubs in for washing. Then again…he wasn't exactly a social butterfly either.

She was top of her game. No one came more highly recommended in her field of pediatric physio than she did.

Snap. He was up there in the top-rated limb specialists.

She was opinionated.

Snap again.

Fair dos to the woman, she hadn't blinked once when he'd all but marched her to an empty room a few doors down from Adao's and wheeled on her.

He counted to ten in time with her heartbeat before he'd steadied his own enough to speak.

"So." He crossed his arms and tipped his head toward Adao's room. "What was that all about?"

She gave her head a quick shake as if she didn't understand.

He waited. His failsafe technique.

Far more effective than saying the myriad of things he could have:

"There's only one person in charge in that room and it's me."

Not his style.

"Since when is a physio a psychiatrist?"

Ditto. He wasn't into tearing people down, but he did like explanations for outbursts.

The seconds ticked past.

Naomi threw a quick look over her shoulder,

stuffed her hands in the pockets of her Hope Hospital hoodie then said, "Okay. Fine. I just feel for the little man, you know?"

He loved the way she said "feel"—even if it was a verb he didn't include in his own vocabulary. She said it as if the word had heft. Gravitas, even. As if it *meant* something.

What a thing to have all that emotion churning round in your chest. Way too much extra baggage to haul around the hospital if he wanted to do his job properly. If he professed to know one solitary thing about himself it was this: Finn Morgan did not do baggage.

Ha!

He coughed into his hand to hide a self-deprecating smirk.

If his ex-wife could read his thoughts, she would've pounced on them like a mouse on cheese.

One of the last things she'd said to him before he'd left his past where it belonged was that he was *"Made* of baggage." And one day? "One day," she'd said to him, "all of that baggage will tumble open and wreak havoc with the man you keep telling yourself you are."

How about that for a "let's keep it friendly" farewell.

On a good day he recalled her "prophesy" as tough love.

On bad days? On bad days he tried not to think of her at all.

He shifted his weight off his knee and brought his thoughts back to Adao and Naomi. "How do you 'feel' for him? Are you from Kambela?"

"No, I'm…" She started to say something then pressed her lips together and started again. "I know what it's like to arrive somewhere new and feel…overwhelmed. Not know who to trust."

"Oh, I see. So you're the only one he can trust here, is that what you're saying?"

Why was he being so confrontational? She was clearly doing what any employee of Hope Children's Hospital should be doing: Holding the patient's needs first and foremost in their mind. At all times.

Take it down a notch, man. She's trying to do right by the kid.

He shrugged the tension out of his shoulders and adopted what he hoped was a less confrontational pose. "I see what you're saying. The kid's been through a lot. But the one person he's got to trust is me." He let it sink in a minute. He was the one who would be holding the scalpel tomorrow. He was the one who would be changing Adao's life forever.

"You're the one who will help him live. I'm the one who's going to help him rebuild his life," Naomi shot back.

Wow. The pronouncement was so loaded with barbs he could take personally he almost fell back a step. Good thing he didn't take workplace slanging matches personally.

The surgery and recovery Adao required was a step-by-step process. And they weren't anywhere near rehab. No point in popping on rose-colored glasses at this stage. Whether she liked it or not, Adao had a *long* road of recovery ahead of him, and the first step was the operating table. Finn's operating table.

"You got the order right," Finn said. "Life first."

And that was the simple truth of the matter.

Naomi didn't respond verbally. But the pursed lips followed by a swift inhalation told him all he needed to know. She knew the facts as well as she did. She just didn't like them.

"C'mon." He steered her, one hand pressed to the small of her back, toward Adao's room. "All the basics should be taken care of right now. How 'bout you sit in while I talk Adao through his first twenty-four hours here at Hope?"

If she was surprised, Naomi masked it well. If she noticed he dropped his hand from her back about as quickly as he'd put it there, she made no sign of it either. As if the moment had never happened.

The tingling in his fingers spoke a different story. When he'd touched her? That flame in his core had tripled in size.

Leaning against the doorframe, having refused Finn's invitation to join him, Naomi had to silently admit the truth.

She was impressed.

As cranky and gruff as Finn was with her... with Adao?...he was gentle, calm and capable of explaining some incredibly complicated facts in a way that didn't patronize or confuse. When Adao spoke or asked questions, she recognized the same lilting accent she'd acquired when learning English from American missionaries or aid workers. Hers, of course, was softened by years in the UK and was now predominantly British English. His was still raw—lurching between the musical cadence of his mother tongue and wrestling with all the new English words.

"We can go over all of this again," Finn was saying, "whenever you want. But the main thing is we're here to help. Okay, little man? Anything you need?"

Adao shook his head now, his small head and shoulders propped up on the big white pillows. He was a collection of bandages with little bits of his brown skin peeking out at intervals. And his eyes...those big brown eyes rimmed with tears...spoke volumes.

Fear. Bewilderment. Loneliness.

He nodded at Finn but said nothing.

She got that.

The silence.

Admitting there was something or someone you missed so much you thought your heart might stop beating was as good as admitting a part of you wished it would. And despite the anxiety creasing his sweet little brow, she also saw fight in him. He wouldn't be here otherwise.

She ached to go to him. Be by his side. Tell him all the things she wished she had been told when she'd arrived in the UK. That these were good people. And while they weren't family...

Her eyes unexpectedly misted over as Finn and Adao did a big fist, little fist bump.

You couldn't ever replace family. Could you?

Finn crossed to her.

"I think it's time we let him get some rest." Finn tipped his head toward the staffroom. "His minder from the charity is just getting some coffee. She'll stay with him tonight. The chair in the corner converts to a bed, so...we'd best leave him to settle in quietly." He gave her a weighted look. "As you suggested."

Nothing like having your own words come back to bite you in the bum.

He was right, of course. And Adao was in the best possible place. But leaving the little boy was tugging at a double-wide door to her heart she'd long jammed shut. It felt wrong.

"Now," Finn mouthed, when the woman from the charity appeared from round the corner and Naomi's gaze inevitably skidded back in Finn's direction as if he were some sort of homing beacon. It was madness, considering Finn Morgan was the last set of arms she'd throw herself into if she needed comforting. It would be like skipping up to a hungry grizzly bear and asking if he minded if they shared a den. Not. Going. To. Happen.

He had his hand on her elbow and was filling up the rest of the space in the doorframe.

There it was again. That cotton and forest scent. And something extra. She looked up into his slate-colored eyes as if they would give her the answer she needed.

Her heart pounded against her ribcage when it did.

That other scent?

Pure male heat.

Naomi scooped her keys off the ground for a second time.

What had got into her?

She blew out a slow breath, waited until the cloud dissipated, then put the key in the lock and turned it.

See? There.

All she needed to do was blank any thoughts of Finn Morgan and— *Doh!*

There went the keys again. At least she was inside this time.

She jogged up the stairs to her flat, opened the interior door, flicked on the lights and popped her keys into the wooden bowl that rested on the small table she had at the front door.

Home.

She grinned at it.

The studio flat was dinky, but she loved it. Her cocoon. A twenty-minute walk from the hospital. Fifty if she took a run along the river on the way, which, let's face it, was every day. Going to the river had become a bit of a pilgrimage. If only one day she would come back from the river and find everything was—

If only nothing.

She toed off her trainers—against her own advice!—and pushed her door shut with her elbow.

Brightly lit. Simply furnished. Secure. Two floors above a bookshop/coffee shop that catered to students and, as such, was open all night. All the things she needed to get to sleep at night.

She shrugged out of her padded gilet then pulled her hoodie, her long-sleeved T-shirt and her wool camisole off, all but diving into her flannel jimjams that she'd laid out on the radiator when she'd left in the morning.

The one thing about England she'd failed to get used to was the cold. This winter was particularly frigid. Rumors of a white Christmas were swirling around the hospital like...like snowflakes.

She gave herself a wry grin in the bathroom mirror as she let warm water run over her freezing fingers. At least the sub-zero temperatures helped keep her heart on ice.

She shivered, thinking of that hot, intense flare of heat she'd seen in Finn's normally glacial gaze.

Did it mean that he...? No. The man was like a snapping turtle. Don't do this. Do that. Not here. There. Me right. You wrong.

She thought of his athletic build, his bearlike presence. Maybe he was more... Abominable Snowman than snapping turtle. Could one make love to a yeti?

She gave her head a shake. Clearly she'd lost a few brain cells on the cold walk home. Even if Finn wrapped a ribbon round his heart and handed it to her on a velvet cushion... *Pah-ha-ha-ha!* Can you imagine?

She tugged on her wool-lined slipper boots, padded across to her tiny strip of a kitchen and opened the fridge.

Yup! Forgot to go shopping. Again.

She stared at the handful of condiments she'd bought in yet another failed moment of "I'll invite someone over" and wondered what it would be like to open up her fridge and know that she'd be making a meal for herself and her family. She closed the refrigerator door along with the thoughts.

Being in a relationship wasn't on the cards for her. Each time she'd tried...*whoomp.* Up had gone the shields holding court round her heart.

She laughed into the silence of her flat.

At last! She'd found something she and Finn had in common.

Now all she had to do was find a way to get along.

CHAPTER FOUR

"Did you manage to get some sleep?" Finn looked over at Adao's case worker from the charity when all he elicited from the little boy was an uncertain mini-shrug.

"He slept a little." She gave the boy's creased forehead a soothing stroke with the backs of her fingers before crossing to him and holding out a sheaf of paperwork. "I'm Sarah Browning, by the way. I'm afraid we're short-staffed and I've got to get a move on." Her features creased apologetically.

Finn nodded and took the paperwork. "Not a problem. We've got plenty of folk who are looking forward to spending time with this little guy. Myself included." He looked over at Adao for any sign of emotional response.

Nothing.

Hardly surprising considering what he'd been through. It was a shame the charity's financial reach couldn't have extended to bringing at least one of the family members over. Then again…from what he'd read prior to the boy's arrival, both the mum and dad worked and his teenage sister was still in school, so… not easy to uproot an entire family.

He slapped the papers against his thigh. Too loudly, from the sharp look the charity worker sent him.

"Right." Finn gave Sarah his best stab at a smile. "Looks like you need to get a move on and I need to assess Adao before we get him into surgery this afternoon."

He went to the doorway and called to the small team of doctors and nurses who would be in surgery with him. "Righto, mateys. Let's get a move on, shall we?" A twinge of déjà vu hit him as the team moved toward the door as one solid mass. Naomi had been right. Too many people standing around Adao might render the kid less responsive than he already was.

"Hey, mate." He looked Adao in the eye. "We've got a bunch of people who are going to come in, but they're all here to help you, yeah? We're all on your side."

The little boy pursed his lips and then nodded. He understood. He didn't like it. But it wasn't exactly as if he was in a position to argue.

Finn's heart went out to the little man, but he needed to keep his cool. Clean, clear precision was what was required when he stepped into surgery today. Anything less wasn't acceptable.

Finn went out into the corridor as the team crowded into the smallish room to hear the details of Adao's case and help set up a battle plan for the afternoon's surgery.

Battle plan.

The cruel irony of it...

He heard a laugh and his eyes snapped to the nurses' station. The hairs on his arms prickled to attention and a deep punch of heat rocket-launched itself exactly where it didn't belong.

Dammit.

Last night's gym session clearly hadn't drilled his body's organic response to her out of his system.

Who knew a woman's scent could linger in the physio gym hours after she'd left the hospital?

He did, that's who. He didn't know if she wore perfume or body spray or what...he just knew that jasmine and vanilla were forever lost to him as plain old smells now.

"Mr. Morgan? I was wondering if I could have a quick word."

"Yes?" Grabbing his work tablet from the counter, he looked back up at her then instantly regretted it. Those dark eyes of hers were blinking away his brusque greeting as her hands rose to tug on each of her loosely woven, below-the-shoulder plaits.

They made her look fun.

And sexy as hell.

"Hi. Um…hello." Naomi stepped behind the high counter of the nurses' station, putting a physical buffer between them.

So she felt it too. Or was avoiding the "back off" daggers he was sending her way.

Fair enough. He'd hardly been Prince Charming last night. Or the day before that. Or…yup. Patterns. He saw it, but she messed with his focus and he didn't like his highly honed "this way trouble lies" vibes being messed with.

"What is it? I've got the team waiting for the pre-surgery assessment."

"I…um…" Something flickered in those

dark brown eyes of hers. Had he ever noticed they were flecked with gold?

Yeah. Just like she'd probably noticed his eyes were flecked with amber when the sun hit them. Not. Can it, Romeo. Those days are over.

"You coming in to listen or is the idea to break up the assessment mid-flow with more of your touchy-feely stuff?"

Why are you being such an ass?

Naomi's dark irises flashed with disbelief at his narky question. Even the ward sister shot him a sharp look. Great. Just what he needed. More fodder for the nurses to continue the tar-and-feather job they no doubt had begun in the break room.

And it was deserved.

All of it.

If Naomi turned on her heel and marched straight up to HR to report him, he wouldn't blame her.

He was at war with himself and no one was coming out the victor. His body wanted one thing, his head wanted another. His heart was being yanked from side to side and therein lay the crux of the matter.

Good thing he didn't do feelings. Or poetry, for that matter. Ode to a smashed-up, battered heart didn't have much of a ring to it.

To his surprise, and the charge nurse's, Naomi shook her head and gave him a gentle smile. "No, no. Please. Go ahead. I'm here to listen."

He gave her a curt nod. "Fine." Then he turned and walked into Adao's room.

"Looks like someone's gunning for a lump of coal in his stocking this Christmas."

Naomi willed herself to smile back at Amanda, the charge nurse, who was always ready with a quip. She could tell from Amanda's expression it looked as forced as it felt. It appeared all she needed to do to rile Finn Morgan was exist!

"Don't let him get to you, Naomi." Amanda gave her shoulders a quick squeeze as she handed her a mini gingerbread man. "We all bank on you and your sunny smile to keep us cheery, so don't give him the satisfaction of taking it away."

Naomi blinked in surprise.

"Don't look so shocked. We're all in awe of your energy."

"My energy?"

"Of course. Who else around here runs up the stairs after running to work and running round with patients all day. Just watching you is exhausting! We all call you the Fizzy Physio." Amanda laughed then leaned in close after giving a swift conspiratorial look around the reception area. "He's all grizzly on the outside and perfectionist on the inside. We've all decided there's a bit of gold in there somewhere but someone has yet to unearth it."

"Unearth it how?"

"The usual way." She performed a teensy sexy dance. "Romance."

Naomi blew a raspberry. As if. The last thing she could ever imagine Finn engaging in was a hospital romance. She winced. She was hardly one to judge.

"Maybe you could be the one to tease it out of him."

"What? Me?" A solitary laugh escaped. "I don't think so." Her eyes did a quick flick in his direction and in the millisecond she allowed herself to look at him she did think...well... he's not *all* bad.

"Hmm. Well, it's not exactly as if anyone catches him out on the razzle anyway." Amanda picked up a tablet and started tapping away with some patient information.

"What do you mean?"

"He never—and I mean never ever—accepts invitations to go out. And that's weird."

"It's not that weird," Naomi said, instantly realizing she was defending her own penchant for staying in at night. She'd gone out for the odd night, but had always sneaked off early. She never seemed to be able to let herself go the way the other women did.

"'Course it is!" Amanda protested. "New hospital. New staff. New chance to meet friends, fall in love if you want— Oh. Uh-oh! Did I hit a nerve?"

"Ha! No."

Yes. Definitely yes.

Amanda inspected her for a minute then grinned as if she'd pocketed a state secret.

"What are you doing up here on the surgical floor anyway? Adao won't be ready for physio until after the surgery."

"I know. I— Well, I…"

Amanda's entire demeanor changed, her expression softening with compassion. "Ah. One of *those*."

Naomi bit down on the inside of her cheek. Hard. She needed that "Fizzy Physio" cover more than anyone here knew.

"Hey. Don't worry. Some of them get to you more than others." Amanda tipped her head toward Adao's room. "Just don't let Mr. All Work and No Play rile you. He's all right as long as you wear your crocodile skin when you're in the same room."

"Got it." Naomi smiled, relieved to have dodged more questions about Adao.

"Collins!" Finn barked from the doorway. "Are you going to join us or are you too busy with the gossip brigade?"

Amanda gave her hand a quick squeeze then nudged her toward the room with a whispered, "Don't worry, his bark is worse than his bite."

She followed Finn into the room, staying put at the doorway as he shouldered his way through the seven or eight physicians and nurses already around the little boy's bed.

Finn obviously didn't want her there but that

was tough. She'd seen Adao arrive last night and wanted him to know she would be there for him when he came out of surgery. After all, she and Adao would be working intimately together in rehab.

Rehab wasn't just tough physically.

It put many of her young patients through an emotional mangle. Adao was bound to have a truckload of emotions come in wave after wave as they worked together.

He had numerous cuts and nicks on his face. None were so brutal they had blinded him or reduced his facial motor function, but there would be scars. Inside and out.

"Right, everyone!" Finn gave a theatrical throat-clearing noise as he took pole position at the head of Adao's bed. "Adao Weza, seven years old and fresh in from Kambela on the west coast of Africa."

He gave the boy a nod and...well, she guessed it was a smile. Hard to tell, coming from someone who clearly had gone to the Neanderthal School of Social Skills.

Ugg. Me surgeon. Me have no feelings. Ugg.

Naomi tucked herself behind one of the junior doctors so she could hide her smile as she pictured Finn wielding a wooden club while wearing a caveman's leopardskin ensemble.

She could still see Adao but was just out of that steel-gray eyeline of Finn's. Meeting his piercing gaze was too unnerving when all she really wanted to do was focus on the little boy.

Perhaps Finn was every bit as upset by Adao's case as she was and this whole Cro-Magnon act was just that...an act. He definitely wasn't the touchy-feely type.

She gave her head a quick shake, her plaits shifting from shoulder to shoulder as she did so, looking up only to catch Finn glaring at her before he rattled off the facts.

Adao had been in a field when his playmate had stepped on an anti-personnel mine. The mine had instantly exploded. She pressed her eyes closed tightly as he continued. She knew, more than most, how easily landmines could go off. The rebels in her own country had taken particular pleasure in littering them throughout the small vegetable patches most families had behind their homes. Two-for-ones, they called them. The blasts knocked out the women and the food supply in one cruel blast. Each morning she and her sister had gone out to the vegetable patch with a long stick, poking and prodding any upturned earth…hoping… praying that today they would be safe.

"Am I boring you, Miss Collins?"

"Sorry." Naomi snapped to attention, horrified to see all the eyes in the room were on her. "No. Not at all."

"Then can you please indulge me and the rest of the team with what you would see as the best solution for the tissue damage Adao has sustained?" Finn's eyes were bright with challenge.

If only he knew. She hadn't been blocking out his words, she'd been trying to block out her own memories.

She pressed her heels into the floor and looked him straight back in the eye. "Well, as you know, I am a physio, not a surgeon, but my understanding is that free tissue transfer can aid with repairing extensive soft tissue defects if the limb has endured serial debridement."

Finn nodded. He wanted her to continue.

Murmurs of curiosity rippled through the team as they cleared a little space around her.

"After a series of pre-operative diagnoses—'

"Which diagnosis? Be specific."

He wanted specifics? Fine. He could have specifics.

She rattled off the list of tests she knew Adao would have to go through prior to surgery—all of which were geared toward finding just how much of his arm they could save while providing his body with optimum chances of healing. She concluded with the overall goal, "The greater the blood flow, the better the healing."

Finn nodded. "So we're looking at measuring his blood flow. What else?" He scanned the room."

"Oxygen tension," said a nurse.

"Good. What else?"

"If the pressure is zero, no healing will occur," jumped in one of the surgical interns. "Ideally, we're looking for the pressure to read higher than forty mils."

"Excellent." Finn scanned the room. "What else?"

Naomi's eyes flicked to Adao's. The pain and fear she saw in them as the medical terminology flew across the room pounded the air out of her chest. A fierce, primal need to do everything she could for this little boy seized every cell in her body, giving her the extra jolt of courage to cut in again.

Finn had been through a trauma of some sort. Surely he had some compassion for this little boy.

Eyes locked with Finn's, she suddenly felt as though they were two prey animals, each wondering who would be the first to pounce. "What's most important for Adao is getting him to a place where he can begin gentle physio—'

"Yes. Fine." Finn cut her off. "We're not there, yet."

"But…" Wasn't giving Adao something to hope for every bit as helpful as doing a skin fluorescence study to measure his microcirculation? He was a little *boy*! A terrified little boy!

"But nothing. We've got the theatre booked in a few hours' time, Miss Collins. He's got to be as strong as possible going into surgery and time's awasting."

Finn gave the back of his tablet a few swift raps with his knuckles and carried on talking his team through the finer points of the surgery, fastidiously ignoring Naomi's shocked expression.

How could he have done that? Interrupting her was one thing, but making that noise?

He didn't even notice how Adao had started at the sound, but she had.

The sharp rat-a-tat-tat had the same effect on her nerves as it obviously did on Adao's.

To them it wasn't knuckles on plastic.

It was the sound of gunfire.

Finn felt Naomi's presence up in the viewing gallery before he confirmed it with a quick sidelong glance.

Her fingers were in prayer position up at that full mouth of hers. A line furrowed between her brows as he meticulously worked his way through the initial phase of the operation before he began shaping what remained of Adao's arm in preparation for a prosthetic device.

What was it with her and this kid? It wasn't as if the hospital hadn't had amputees before. It was, after all, his specialty.

He blanked the gallery viewing room and returned his focus to Adao's small form.

"Skin temperature's slightly different." He

nodded to the nurse by the instrument tray. He really didn't want to have to take off more than he had to, but he knew better than most that providing a solid foundation for the prosthesis was crucial.

There'd been no way to save the elbow joint. A layperson could've figured that out. But he had been hoping for an elbow disarticulation rather than the more blunt approach of a proximal amputation. By employing a fastidious millimeter by millimeter approach, he prepared Adao's arm for separation at the joint, thereby providing a solid platform for his prosthetic device. He'd read about some electric elbow prostheses that could potentially set the boy up for a relatively normal life. He might not become a pianist, but...

With any luck, he'd be ready for some gentle physiotherapy in a handful of days.

An image of Naomi massaging Adao's shoulder with her slender fingers blinded him for an instant. Blinded him because it wasn't Adao he was picturing receiving her sympathetic care. It was him.

It may have been a millisecond but it was a millisecond too long.

"Clear the gallery!"

His growl of frustration sent everyone from the gallery flying. If there was one thing that held true in Hope Children's Hospital it was that the surgeon got what the surgeon wanted when it came to offering a child the best care possible.

Pop music?

No problem.

A favorite scrubs cap?

Same again.

A gallery free of invested onlookers?

That was fine, too. As long as everything came out good in the end.

Muscles, connective tissue, skin all played a role in creating the foundation of what would be Adao's arm from now on.

Sometimes he thought he got the easy part and the physio was actually the one who took the brunt of the patient's pain. Thank God his own physiotherapist had been unfazed by blue language because he had painted that therapy gym the color of a sky heading toward the blackest of midnights for his first few sessions. If by "few" he meant six months. Anyone and everyone who'd crossed his path—and that included family—had been soundly pushed away. The only way he'd survived those dark days had been with grim determination.

Phantom limb pain.

A poor-fitting prosthesis.

Infection.

A second surgery.

He'd had them all.

And he hadn't wanted anyone who claimed to love him within earshot. If ever he'd felt like a wounded animal—made of little else other than rage and fear—it had been then.

It was what had driven him to retrain as a pediatric surgeon after he'd finally got out of rehab and had pushed his past as far away as he could. No one—especially children—should have to go through what he had. And under his watch they wouldn't.

Which was why he did the hard part—the part that required a methodical, emotionless approach—and positive, forward-thinking people like Naomi did the aftercare.

Two or three back-achingly painful hours later he stood back from the surgery table, knowing he had done his best.

"Good work, everyone." He pulled off his surgical cap and threw it in the laundry bin by the swinging theatre doors. "Make sure I'm paged when he wakes up, yeah? One of you stay with him at all times. I don't want the little guy on his own. Not tonight."

His eyes shifted up to the empty gallery.

Idiot.

He should've let her stay.

His gut told him she was the one Adao should be seeing as he blinked his eyes open when he woke from the anesthetic.

His head told him to just butt out and carry on as always. No attachments. No guilt. He was already dragging around enough of the latter, thank you very much, and the last thing he was going to do was add a leggy physio to the list of people he'd wronged.

That list was already full up.

CHAPTER FIVE

NAOMI BURIED HER face in the dog's curly coat and gave him a hug. Much to her delight, he sat back on his haunches and put his paws on her shoulders as if giving her a proper hug.

"He's gorgeous!" She looked up at his handler… Alana, was it?…and opted to ask the surgeon beside her instead. "What's his name, Marco?"

"Doodle," Marco Ricci answered, as if it was patently obvious that the golden-brown labradoodle should be called Doodle. The surgeon gave the pooch's head a quick scrub then wished Alana well.

The pair of them watched as Doodle and his trainer made their way along and out of the hospital corridor.

"Alice thinks he's brilliant. Would use him for all her patients if she could. Whether they needed them or not," Marco said, as they disappeared round the corner.

"Wow." High praise indeed, coming from Alice Baxter, one of the most driven, dedicated surgeons she'd met at Hope Hospital. Then again, having recently fallen in love with Marco, it was little wonder Alice was loving life and seeing the positive side of everything.

Unlike Finn Morgan...the Caveman of Doom.

Naomi shook the thought away—along with the image of Finn back in his caveman togs— and pulled out the small notebook she always carried with her. "That sounds amazing. I think I know someone who would really benefit from a therapy dog session."

Finn, for one.

Might help the man grow a heart.

Not that she was still smarting from being kicked out of the surgery. Or was acutely aware that she was the reason it happened. Flashes of connection didn't strike like lightning then just fade away. They burnt.

"Who's it for?" Marco asked. His tone was friendly. Curious.

Unlike Finn, who would've flung the question at her combatively.

Urgh! Stop thinking about Finn!

"Adao. You know, the boy in from Kambela for an arm amputation."

"Yes. Of course. Yesterday, wasn't it? I heard the operation went well."

Naomi gave her best neutral nod. "That's what I hear."

"Sounds like we all *heard* and none of us *saw.* Rumor has it the Beastie Man of Orthopedics kicked everyone out of the observation gallery." He laughed as an idea struck him. "You sure you aren't booking the therapy dog for him?"

"Positive." The more space between Mr. Finn Morgan and her, the better. She'd popped into Adao's room a couple of times after checking the coast was clear. The first time he'd been asleep. The second she had given his shoulders a gentle massage, eyes glued to the door in case she needed to make a swift exit. Official physio wasn't meant to start until tomorrow, but when she'd drawn up enough courage to go to Finn's office and check if that was still the plan, he'd already gone for the night.

The deflation she'd felt at not finding him

there had shocked her. It wasn't as if she'd been actually looking forward to seeing him.

Well.

No one liked conflict.

Besides, the man was clearly battling demons on his own. She dealt with hers by putting on an extra-cheery façade and pretending she didn't have a past and he... Well, he growled at people like a grumpy grizzly. So to each his own. Who was she to judge?

"If you're after booking some time with Doodle and Alana, the woman you're after is..." Marco rocked back on his heels and did the air guitar version of a drumroll. "Evie Cooper! The source of all wisdom at Hope Hospital."

Naomi smiled. Evie. Of course.

"I'll go hunt her down."

"Two guesses as to where you'll find her."

"NICU or PICU?" Naomi smiled. Evie was not only the resident elf, she was the hospital's resident baby whisperer. The whole staff had swelled with pride when word had gone out she was going to fulfil a lifelong dream of finishing her nursing degree.

"Or wherever Mr. Walker might happen to be." Marco smiled then glanced at his watch.

"Speaking of which, there is a certain blond surgeon who's no doubt wondering where I am. Good luck with the therapy dog. Hopefully he'll be the secret weapon you were hoping for."

She gave him a wave and headed for the stairwell, jogging up the stairs to see if she could find Evie before she headed off.

Everyone's schedules had gone absolutely haywire with the arrival of the holiday season. No one was waiting for the first of December to get their holiday groove on. It was as if the opening gala at the hospital had unleashed an entire year's worth of magic fairy dust. Half the hospital seemed to be falling in love and decorating Christmas trees or piling nurses' stations with gingerbread men while cross-checking diaries that drinks dates, department dinners and Secret Santas were all accounted for.

And the other half?

Her own evening diary was as pristine as a snow-covered field. Not that she minded. Much.

The truth was, she had only ever dated men with whom she'd known she had no future.

They had tended to be serious, more interested in science than sex. Which was fine with her.

Being with someone...being *happy* with someone...*physical* with someone...it didn't seem fair. Not when everyone she'd loved had had their lives cut so short.

On the flipside, she saw just how unfair life was every day at work and, for the most part, her young patients just got on with it. They accepted that life threw grenades at all sorts of people. There was no rhyme or reason to it. That was just the way it was. So they chose to focus on the positive.

She did on the outside. But inside? It felt as though she was frozen. And in order to survive she needed to stay that way.

When she pushed through to the NICU reception area there was scarcely a soul about.

She looked at her watch. It was after seven. It explained why Finn hadn't been in his office. Not that she'd seen him wandering round the hospital after hours, as she had a tendency to do. What sort of life did he lead after hours if he wasn't part of the "meet for a drink" set? Was he hacking piles of wood to bits with a huge, hand-honed axe?

Or needlepointing tapestries of intricate flower patterns to help him with the delicate art of surgery at which he so clearly excelled?

Pah! Yeah, right.

"Can I help you?" The nurse manager, Janine, looked up from her computer screen where she was updating some charts.

"I was just looking for Evie. I wanted to see if I could get some contact details for Doodle." She laughed and corrected herself. "Alana, his handler, I mean."

"Evie's gone for the night, I'm afraid."

Naomi must have looked downcast at the news because Janine quickly added, "You know, a bunch of the nurses have headed down to the White Hart. If you're looking for something to do..."

Naomi pretended to consider the offer. Maybe it would be a good way to distract her from her thoughts. "It's just off the King's Parade, right?"

"That's the one! Go on," Janine urged. "They're a friendly group. They'd love to have you join them. I think the city's even turned on the Christmas lights so it'll be a lovely walk." She peered over the edge of the nurses' station at Naomi's "uniform" of trainers and athletic wear. "Or cycle? Or run?"

"Walk sounds nice." Naomi smiled. They had turned on the lights. She actually lived nearby and had heard all of the oohs and ahhs as the lights had been switched on, followed by a good hour of excited chatter and laughter.

It would do her good. Even if she just went to see the lights. Give her a reminder of life outside the hospital. She looked down at her trainers. Not really going-out gear, but...why not give it a go? Who knew, maybe she'd take a new route and discover something else about Cambridge to tell Adao about when they began their proper treatment the next day.

Twenty minutes later Naomi was lost. With the medieval twists and turns of the city center and all the twinkling lights, she'd allowed her thoughts to drift away and had lost track of where she was.

She could hear laughter and the sound of a ball game being played nearby. A group of children were obviously playing footie, with someone teasing and cajoling them from the spirited yelps and guffaws traveling round the corner. A sports center, maybe? A small green?

She made a promise to herself to ask the first person she laid eyes on. What she didn't expect was to discover the laughing, fun-loving man powering along the floodlit football pitch with a child hanging off each of his well-built arms was Finn Morgan.

She froze, unable to reconcile the dedicated curmudgeon she knew from the hospital with this bright-eyed, chuckling human climbing frame! He looked positively alight with joy.

Spurring herself into action, she turned to go just as he lifted his head and met her eyes. Their gazes crashed together and locked tight.

Naomi's heart pounded against her chest as she saw his eyes brighten, then just as quickly turn dull with recognition as the smile faded from his lips.

"Naomi! Hang on a minute."

She looked as surprised as Finn felt. And the look of dismay on her face when he had let his features fall into a frown had touched something deep within him.

He knew hurt.

He knew pain.

And he'd caused both in Naomi.

"Don't go." He scanned his ragtag team of footie mates looking up at him for guidance. He'd never brought a "stranger" to sports night. Hell. He'd not brought anyone anywhere for years.

"Do you think she wants some hot chocolate?" asked Ashley. She was the undisputed leader of the group. One crook of her arm and every single one of those kids followed in her wake.

He glanced back across at Naomi, who was still rooted to the spot.

Yeah. She'd "caught him" in his private place, but it *was* a public playing field. That, and he really had to do something to break the ever-increasing tension building between them. There were only so many alternative routes a man whose patients all required physio in a hospital with one exquisitely talented and beautiful-without-knowing-it physiotherapist could take.

"C'mon." He waved her over, two scrawny six-year-olds still hanging from each arm and—he looked down—yup, two kids on his good leg. At least they had the sense to leave his "robot" leg alone.

The uncertainty in her eyes got to him. He wasn't an ogre.

Well.

Not all the time.

"It's freezing out. Let's get you a cup of hot chocolate. What do you say, lads and ladettes? Hot chocolate all round before I beat you all in the second half?"

Cheers erupted round him and he couldn't resist joining in. These kids were awesome. Some of them had special needs. Some of them were just lonely. For all the beauty and brains Cambridge had on offer, there was also a poorer, lonelier side. Parents working overnight caretaker shifts. Single mums earning just enough to pay the rent and not quite enough to get food on the table. More latchkey kids than there should be. More pain than there should be.

If he could put a two-hour dent in their loneliness and give their cheeks a flush from a bit of a run-around and get some healthy grub into their bellies, then he was all for it. The hot chocolate was just a bonus. So week in, week out, this was his home away from home.

He probably needed them as much as they needed him. They kept him from falling back into that pit of self-loathing that he'd used to ill effect. It had turned out that driving everyone you loved away had a flipside. You were on your own when the demons attacked.

He looked across at Naomi and took an invisible punch to the chest when her features lit up with a genuine smile. A grin, actually. Had he noticed she had dimples before?

Damn. That smile of hers pierced right through to bits of him that hadn't so much as shown a flicker of interest in years. He was no monk, but even his home—a houseboat he'd picked up when he'd been retraining in London—was something he could unmoor and just…float away.

It's hot chocolate, you idiot. Not a proposal.

He gently shook the boys off him, doing his best to avoid Naomi's inquisitive looks. His hand was itching to reach out to the small of her back, see if touching her with fourteen layers of clothes on still elicited fireworks. Instead, he grabbed a little curly-haired moppet under his arm and gave him a quick fist bump. That sort of contact he could deal with. "All right, matey. Time to learn a little something about showing some hospitality."

Finn steered everyone directly toward the sports center's kitchen, which had its own outside entrance. There was a game going on in the gym he didn't want to interrupt.

"All right, everyone. To your stations!"

The children all ran to their pre-assigned spots and Finn couldn't help but feel a surge of pride. Not because he wanted to show off in front of Naomi or anything—well, maybe a little—but it was nice to see these kids so keen to please. When he'd met them, most had lacked the social skills that would help them on a day-to-day basis.

"Excuse me, miss?"

Finn grinned. His star "pupil," Archie, was standing in front of Naomi with a little pad of paper in his hand as if he worked at a Michelin-starred restaurant. "Please, miss. May I take your hot chocolate order?"

Naomi squatted down so she was about the same height as Archie.

It was a nice move. Not many people treated these kids with respect. He shouldn't have been surprised Naomi would be one of them.

"What are my options?" she asked, her eyes twinkling with delight.

"Well..." Archie looked up at Finn with a flash of panic on his face. There weren't really options. It was hot chocolate or...well, hot chocolate. Squash never really got a look-in this time of year.

"Why don't you ask the lady—whose name is Miss Collins—if she'd like it hot or cold, and whether or not she might like marshmallows on top?"

"There are marshmallows?" Archie looked around at his playmates in disbelief. A ripple of excited whispers turned into a sea of high fives and whoops when Finn reached up above one of the cupboards where he'd stashed a tin of Christmas-tree-shaped marshmallows and revealed them to the children.

Wide-eyed, Naomi reached to the floor to steady herself.

What? A man wasn't allowed to indulge in a bit of home economics?

A soldier—an *ex*-soldier—had to feed himself. Especially when he'd told everyone who was dear to him to bugger off.

Turned out water biscuits and cheese did not maketh the man.

"But, Finn!" Archie shook his hands in exasperation. The kid had Asperger's and always had to get things exactly right before he could move forward on any project. Even putting home-made marshmallows into hot chocolate. "Marshmallows are made from horses' hooves, which also bear a similarity to reindeer hooves, which, if you consider the season—"

"Whoa there, mate." Finn gave his shoulder a reassuring squeeze then lifted one of the little tree-shaped confections and popped it into his mouth. "These little babies are as pure as the driven snow. No horse hooves. No reindeer feet. Get your pen ready. I used vegan gelatin." He ticked off the ingredients on his fingers slowly because he knew Archie would want to write them down. "Water. Sugar. Fairtrade." He threw a look in Naomi's direction, not entirely sure why he cared that she knew he bought Fairtrade, but...whatever.

Proof he had a heart, he guessed. "Icing sugar. Salt and vanilla."

"My mother says sugar is evil," one of the children jumped in.

"Only evil if it's your only food group." And he should know. He'd survived off a stale box of party rings for a week once when his knee had been giving him jip. Weeks like that one had been the beginnings of finding the fight again. The will to live versus survival.

So he'd cracked open a recipe book and— *voilà*. Turned out he could cook.

"Extract or flavoring?" asked Archie.

"Extract. Only the good stuff for you lot."

He reached up again and pulled down another tin, revealing a couple of dozen flapjacks dotted with cranberries and dried apricots and whatever else he'd found in his cupboards before his shift this morning.

Archie cleared his throat and started again. "Miss Collins, would I be able to interest you in one of Cambridge sports club's finest instant hot chocolate sachets with a topping of home-crafted marshmallows?"

Naomi gave the ends of her red woolen scarf

a tug and gave a low whistle. "Wow. That's quite an offer. I would be delighted. Now…" she reached out a hand to Archie "…what did you say your name was? Mine's Naomi."

Archie looked up at Finn—a clear plea for permission to shake the pretty lady's hand. Finn nodded.

"Can I make it?" Ashley shot her hand up into the air as far as it would go.

"I don't know, can you?"

"*May* I make it," corrected Ashley. *"Please?"*

"I want to pour the water!" Jimbo—their littlest warrior—leapt to the hot water urn.

"Whoa, there, soldiers. Who's the only man on campus who does the boiling water?"

"You!" all the children shouted, their arms moving as one toward him followed by a little cheer that always cracked him up.

These kids were nuts.

He gave a couple of their sweaty little heads a scrub and as he turned to get to work caught Naomi looking at him with an expression of pure warmth. It disappeared so quickly when she saw he was looking at her it was akin to seeing a falling star.

Little short of a miracle.

* * *

Naomi felt as if she'd walked into an alternate universe.

Finn Morgan made marshmallows and flapjacks?

She tried to picture him wearing a frilly pinafore and oven mitts and came up with… Oh, my, that was all she pictured him in.

Unexpected.

Was that what a glimpse of the "heart of gold" could do to a girl? Turn a man naked in her imagination?

Crikey.

She gave her head a shake and watched as all the children fell into place for what was obviously a finely tuned routine.

The littlest kids pulled out mugs from the lower shelves of the sports center's kitchen. Bigger ones emptied packets of hot chocolate into the mugs—about a dozen all told. One—who seemed to be the mini-matriarch of the pack—slotted herself in and around them to wipe up any stray chocolate powder.

One scuttled up to Finn, who was holding court at the hot-water urn—wise, considering the sign on the metal urn warned that the water was at a boiling temperature at all times—and beckoned to him that he wanted to whisper something in his ear.

Finn knelt down, his eyes shifting up to the ceiling as the little boy cupped his hands round Finn's ear and whispered. Finn's gray eyes traveled to the two mugs in the little boy's hands and said something in a low rumbling voice then tipped his head in Naomi's direction. "Go on."

The little boy shook his head and pressed the mugs into Finn's huge hands. Had she actually noticed how big his hands were?

He rose to his full height and turned to her. *Gulp.*

About as big as the rest of him.

"Miss Collins, would you like the flowery mug or the ladybird mug with a chip in it? Jamie is sorry in advance about the chip, but he can recommend use of the ladybird mug from personal experience." He held them out to her, his features looking as serious as if he were offering her a choice between food for the rest of the month or famine. From the look on Jamie's face, it was on a par.

"Well..." She rose so that she could examine the mugs with proper consideration then gave Jamie a serious nod. "I think I'd like the ladybird mug, if that's all right? Seeing as it comes so highly rated."

The little boy's face nearly split in two with an ear-to-ear grin as he tugged at Finn's shirt. "I told you."

"Well, then, Jamie. Maybe next time you can be brave enough to ask her yourself."

Finn's eyes never left hers as he spoke.

Next time?

She was astonished there was a first time, let alone... Was this an olive branch? His way of saying he was sorry for raking her over the coals at the hospital?

Her heart skipped a beat.

"Finn, look." A little boy came over to him, a marshmallow stuck on each of his index fingers. "I am the ghost of Christmas past!"

And just like that the moment was gone and a new, sillier one had begun. Naomi didn't know whether to be grateful or wistful.

After a few minutes of fussing about with stirring hot chocolates into mugs, doling out the remaining marshmallows and filling kitchen towel squares with a flapjack each, the motley crew were told to head toward the benches in the gym to watch the game.

"Game?"

Finn was shuttling a couple of the children past her as she asked. He dropped an unexpected wink her way.

"You'll see."

When the door to the gym was pushed open, Naomi's eyes widened with delight.

A full-on game of wheelchair basketball was under way complete with heated banter and the non-stop squeak and squeal of wheels on the gym floor. It was mesmerizing.

About a dozen men and women—all in low-slung, wide-angle-wheelchairs—were careening round the gym with all the focused intent of a professional sports team. The atmosphere was absolutely electric.

"All right, chaps and chapesses." Finn issued a few instructions to his team, holding a couple of the steaming mugs of chocolate aloft as they clambered onto the benches to watch the game. From the gleams of excitement in their eyes this was clearly one of the highlights of their night out.

"Want to grab a pew or are you happy here?"

Finn stood beside Naomi, eyes glued to the game, but his presence... It was weird to say, but...it felt like their bodies were *flirting*. Which was completely mental.

Particularly considering she didn't flirt.

She did happy.

She did bubbly.

Flutter her eyelashes and blush like a maiden on the brink of a kiss?

Nope. That wasn't her. Not by a long shot. Because if she were to allow herself to feel good things, she'd inevitably also feel all the bad things, too. And she never wanted to go back there. Because the bad things came cloaked in a bone-deep fear that was too terrifying to even consider confronting. Once had been more than enough.

"Naomi?"

"Happy here, thanks." She took a sip of her chocolate and gave Finn a bright grin. "These marshmallows are amazing. You should sell them at the hospital café."

Finn barked a laugh. "Yeah. I'm sure Theo would love me upping the obesity rate right there on the hospital mezzanine."

Stung, she looked away. "I was hardly suggesting—" She stopped when she felt Finn's hand on her arm, the heat of it searing straight through the triple layers of her outdoor wear.

"Sorry. I didn't mean it like that."

"You never do, do you?"

Finn stepped back and shoved his free hand through that tangle of dark, wavy hair that was all but begging for someone who looked a lot like her to do the same. He never broke eye contact and it took just about all the willpower she possessed not to look away.

"No," he finally said. "I don't."

She had absolutely no reason to believe him. But she did. Something about the flashes of light hitting those steel-gray eyes of his...they spoke volumes. He knew pain. He'd seen it in her eyes just as she'd seen it in his.

At least she now knew they shared some common ground.

His home-made marshmallows were also ridiculously lovely.

Silver linings and all that.

They watched the rest of the game in silence. It was a revelation, watching the hardcore stamina of the wheelchair users in action.

A few minutes later when the whistle was blown he strode across to a man with a pitch-black buzz cut and piercing blue eyes. When both of them looked her way she checked behind her to see what they were looking at. When she looked back, Finn was beckoning her to come over.

"Naomi, I'd like you to meet one of my oldest—'

"Hold up!" The man interrupted. "Longest term—not oldest. Let's keep this accurate." He laughed good-naturedly. "You may continue."

Finn gave his friend a punch in the arm then, still smiling, began the introduction again. "Naomi the Physio meet Charlie the Basketball champ." The change in his tone and demeanor was as warming to her belly as the hot chocolate had been. The two men obviously shared a deep friendship. It was nice to see Finn had so much more to him than gruff bluster and, of course, his incredible reputation as a surgeon.

"Champ?" she asked, truly impressed.

Charlie waved off the title. "Just a couple of regional matches where we beat the pants off the other county teams. Funding's always a problem, but we're hoping to get to the Commonwealth Games next time they come round in the UK. I might be a bit long in the tooth by then, but some of these whippersnappers might still be up to it." He raised his voice and aimed it in their direction. "So long as they all keep listening to my outstanding coaching!"

They sent back their own set of razzes then took the children up on their offer to pour water for them all from the big cooler at the end of the court.

Naomi stood with Charlie as Finn jogged across to oversee the "catering."

"You two together?"

Naomi sucked in her breath and gave an incredulous laugh. "No. I was just walking past and saw them playing. We work together. That's all."

"Huh." Charlie pinned his bright blue eyes on her, as if to say, *I'm more than happy to wait it out until you come clean.*

It didn't take long.

"Honestly. We don't really know each other. The hospital's still relatively new. I do my thing. He does his."

"Yeah, well. I think there might be a little bit o' the lady protesting too much." He chuckled and gave the beads of sweat on his brow a swipe. "I've known Finn a long time and he's never brought anyone in here to see him do his thing before."

"Oh." Seriously? Then again...the man played his cards so close to his chest she sometimes wondered if he'd even seen them. But the only one to ever see him do this amazing work? "Well... I did just happen to be walking past, so..."

"So nothing. I haven't seen him look at anyone like that since the divorce went through."

"Finn was married?"

You could've knocked her over with a feather.

Maybe that explained why his male-female relations were so...rusty. Not that she wanted him to flirt with her or anything. Her eyes traveled across the gym to where a gaggle of children were clamoring to get his attention.

Her heart did a little skippity-hop as their eyes met and he dropped her a quick wink before returning his focus to the children.

Maybe she did.

"Oops. My bad. Open mouth, insert foot!" Charlie grinned unapologetically. "Look. Finn and I go way back. Did our basic training together when we were fresh out of school. Never met anyone who wanted to be an army man more. He started young with everything, precocious upstart that he was." Charlie grinned, his voice warm with genuine affection. "Finn comes from a long line of army men so the second he could enlist he did. Would have lied about it if that sort of thing were possible these days. He married young, too. Then got himself blown up after just a couple of tours in the Middle East, but…" he paused for effect "…not before he saved my life."

What?

An action hero on top of everything else?

Still waters did run deep. At least in the case of Finn Morgan.

"That one?" Naomi pointed across the gym to where Finn was teaching the children how to turn their hands into "pilot goggles" then scanned Charlie's face for signs of a wind-up. "That Finn Morgan saved your life?"

"Too right he did." He gave her a quick glance as if trying to get a gauge on her "combat story readiness."

He wheeled his chair closer to her, looked her straight in the eye and said, "If Finn Morgan hadn't thrown himself on top of me that day, I wouldn't be here."

His tone was enough for Naomi to decipher what he was really saying. Finn Morgan had sacrificed his leg to save his friend's life.

She was about to ask how he'd ended up in the chair but Charlie beat her to the punch. "This happened later. On my next tour. I shipped out while Finn was in rehab. He took it hard. Pushed everyone he loved as far away from him as he could."

Naomi could hardly get her head around the fact that Mr. Grumpy liked to play footie with kids with special needs who he handcrafted seasonal treats for, let alone take in the huge news that not only was he a hero, he was also a broken-hearted divorcee.

"Including his wife?"

It felt such an intimate question to ask.

"Including his wife. She moved on but Finn hasn't. May never forgive himself. He was a seething ball of fury by the time I came back for my own stint in rehab." He shrugged it all off. "He just poured all of his energies into retraining as a pediatric ortho king and...' he blew an imaginary trumpet fanfare from his hand '...*voilà*! Look who is one of the country's top limb specialists. An amazing guy."

This was more than peeling away the layers, like an onion, and finding out there was a diamond in the rough. It was like opening up an enormously intimidating book, only to find the binding and outer layers disguised an enormous and generous heart.

CHAPTER SIX

"FINN! ARE YOU coming along to the Christmas quiz night at the Fox and Hounds?"

Finn scrunched the paper he was drying his hands with into a ball and threw it into the nearby bin. "Nope."

"Now, there's a surprise." Amanda rolled her eyes and laughed good-naturedly. "Don't think a handful of 'nopes' is going to stop me from trying, though."

Finn bit back his usual retort—*good luck with that*—and did his best to give her a better-luck-next-time smile before heading toward the stairs. It wasn't her fault that ducking out of social gatherings was his forte. Especially at this time of year. Everything seemed infused with extra meaning. Intent. He figured Amanda would catch on soon enough. Finn Morgan wasn't a social creature.

So what the hell was he doing, heading down

to the physio gym with a bit of extra fire in his step?

No prizes for guessing the answer there. A sweet, soft smile.

He was hoping for a dose of both.

He may not win Hope Children's Hospital's Most Sociable Doc Award, but it seemed as though he'd done a one-eighty on how he felt about "Naomi run-ins."

The encounter at "his" sports center had changed everything. Letting someone see his private self, the side he allowed to have fun—to *care*—hadn't been the horror show he'd thought it would be.

His world hadn't shattered into bits. He hadn't flared up in anger as he had at his family and wife. His heart still beat. Beat faster, if he was being truly honest.

And, of course, it wasn't just any old someone.

It was Naomi.

Instead of rubbing him up the wrong way, he was experiencing an entirely new breed of agitation.

He actually caught himself *smiling* when their appointments overlapped. Feeling concern when he saw her shoulders tense up in advance of going into Adao's room. Actual, honest-to-God pleasure shot through his veins when she clapped and hugged a patient who'd achieved a new benchmark.

Curiosity teased at his nerve endings. What would it feel like to be on the receiving end of one of those hugs? One of those smiles?

Which was why the deserted physiotherapy gym was getting a bit more after-hours attention from him than usual.

One man. One gym. A perfect night. The best way to pummel all the feelings straight out of his system.

At least that's how it had worked in the "before Naomi" days.

Now that he'd let himself see beyond the beautiful, chirpy façade of hers, and he'd realized she seemed to have every bit as much going on beneath the surface as he did, the gym felt empty if she wasn't there. He'd almost grown to anticipate the quiet way she had of looking at him when he'd been a bit too gruff. The slip of her gaze from his eyes to his hips then his knee on days his leg was giving him jip. The way her cheeks had pinked up when he'd winked at her that night at the gym.

Winked!

What the hell? The last thing his ex would've accused him of was being soppy and yet…each time he walked through the deserted corridors and pushed through the doors to the physio gym, he caught himself hunting for signs of her. A stray clipboard, a little cloud of her perfume, a Hope Hospital hoodie hanging in the small office she used in the corner of the gym.

True, he could've gone to any gym, anywhere in Cambridge, but something about coming to the playground atmosphere of the hospital's physio ward appealed to him. A reminder that if children could push themselves to work harder, achieve their goals, then he could, too.

There were the standard weights and cardio machines any adult physiotherapy center would have. Running machines. Static bicycles. A small set of steps. Massage tables.

But the walls were painted with colorful murals. There was a climbing wall. It was too small for him but it never failed to capture his interest. All of the "rocks" were shaped like dinosaurs. Each time he came down here he traced a new path to the top. And there was also— Ah! A zip wire. And tonight it was in use.

"That's right, Ellie." Naomi was helping a blonde ponytailed girl establish her grip on the bar. "Now, off you go and hold, hold, hold, hold... Hooray!"

Naomi applauded as the young girl—maybe around ten—landed on the huge gym mats at the far end of the zip-wire run.

"Looks like fun."

Naomi snapped to attention, obviously unaware he'd been watching them.

"Yes." She looked at her young charge for confirmation, as if she wasn't entirely sure whether to be happy or wary to see Finn. Wow. That stung. Guess he only had himself to blame.

"What do you think, Ellie? Have you been having fun?"

"Definitely." The girl's eyes shone with pride. "Especially now the distal radius epiphys... epiphysss..."

"Epiphysititis," Naomi and Finn said as one.

Ellie laughed and called out, "Snap!"

Finn just stared. Naomi's eyes were about as deep brown as a woman's eyes could get. A man could get lost in them if he had nothing but time.

She drew in a quick breath and turned back to her young charge.

"I think there should be a rule that until you can say the word, it's not completely gone." Naomi nudged the girl with her hip and Ellie giggled.

"Okay. It's not *gone* gone…but now that the cast is off and I can use my wrist again, I can get back to gymnastics practice, right?"

"Well…that's what we're here to establish, young lady."

The way Naomi's dark eyes twinkled and the corners of her mouth were twitching, it was easy to see she was teasing the girl. He liked that. Having patients think they're playing rather than working was half the battle on the rehabilitation side of things. Naomi was obviously excellent at her job—and enjoyed doing it.

"C'mon, please?" Ellie put her hands into prayer position. "That's the first time I've done the zip wire without letting go."

"A zip wire's one thing. Vaulting is another."

Ellie scanned the room, her eyes alighting on Finn. "I bet I could vault him."

Naomi's eyes widened and a hit of the giggles struck her hard and fast.

"What?" Finn gave a mock frown. "I put Ellie's cast on, if memory serves." With a huge grin, Naomi nodded. "I also took the cast off, which would indicate it was healed. So...tell me, Miss Collins, what exactly is the problem with Ellie here using me as a human vault?"

"Er...health and safety for one?" She crossed her arms playfully and gave him her best what-are-you-going-to-say-to-that-one-pal? look. "Her muscle strength would have deteriorated."

"Not that much!" Ellie pointed at the zip wire as if it was proof she was ready for the next phase. "Look! I can do handstands on the mat, no problem."

They watched and, yes, she could indeed do handstands perfectly well.

"Well." Finn turned to Naomi when Ellie put her hands into prayer position again and gave them both a doleful round of puppy-dog eyes. "I doubt she was planning on vaulting all six foot two inches of me, were you, Ellie?" He pressed himself up to his full height and actually—oh, good grief—he'd actually swelled his chest a bit. Like a cartoon character.

Why are you showboating like this?

Mercifully, Ellie was oblivious to his lame attempt at flirting with Naomi. She was already dragging a mat over alongside the ball pit. "Look, Naomi, I won't do the splits version. I'll just do a simple handspring. If Finn kneels on here..." Ellie eyeballed him for a minute and he tried not to laugh. He'd never really been considered as gymnastics equipment before. Ellie pointed at Finn to relocate himself. Stat. "Mr. Morgan, you have to kneel here and then I'll do a quick run-up on the mats here and when I do the handstand over you, I'll land in the ball pit so it'll be totally safe."

Naomi tilted her head to the side and stared at him. If he thought he was being considered for anything more than a stand-in vaulting horse he would've read something into it. But this was work and it was easy enough to see Naomi's focus was one hundred percent on her patient's safety. As his should be. Which did beg the question...

"You ready, Finn?"

"If we have Naomi's stamp of approval."

Finn and Ellie turned to Naomi as one and the smile that lit up her face at both of their expectant expressions was like the sun emerging from a cloud on a summer's day. Pure light.

Damn, she was beautiful.

"Fine!" She threw up her hands. "Under two conditions. One…" She gave Naomi a stern look. "I will stand by to spot you. And two…" She looked at Finn and then quickly shifted her gaze to his knee. "If you think you're up to it."

He did a squat, as if that was the ultimate proof he could kneel on all fours.

Hmm… That was what her expression said. She drummed her fingers on her lips for a moment then put up a finger. "Hang on a minute." She jogged to the far end of the room and rummaged through a drawer for a minute. She brandished an elasticated wrist brace as if it were a long-sought-after treasure. "Put this on first."

"Thank you, Naomi!" Ellie threw her arms around Naomi then pulled on the brace and eyed Finn with the cool acuity of a girl who knew her way around a competitive gymnastics tournament. "Are you ready, Mr. Morgan?"

"As I'll ever be." He went down on all fours and steadied himself, wondering how the hell he'd gone from wanting a quiet workout on his own to being part of a ten-year-old's gymnastic ambitions.

He looked straight ahead of him to where Naomi had relocated herself to spot Ellie if she needed it.

Her dark eyes shimmered with delight for Ellie as she executed the move to perfection and, much to his satisfaction, when he rose to his full height in front of Naomi, there was an extra flash of pleasure just for him.

After Ellie's mum had come and collected her and she'd been signed off to go on her gymnastics tournament—"using the brace!"—Naomi returned to the gym, surprised to find Finn was still there.

"Did you need anything?" She'd not been alone with him since he'd bitten her head off before Adao's arrival, but seeing him at the sports center the other day seemed to have softened the tension that often crackled between them. Further evidence that gold heart the charge nurse had alluded to wasn't a myth.

"Nope." Finn looked around him as if sizing up the place. "I sometimes sneak down here after hours for a bit of a workout, but having stood in as a human gymnasium was good enough for tonight."

Naomi laughed. "I suspect it wasn't really on a par with your normal workouts."

She saw him start to say something, his eyes alight with fun, and then bite it back, his expression turning back to the thunder face she was more used to.

She turned away so he wouldn't see the disappointment in her eyes. And the shock. Who would've thought a chance sighting at a sports center and a brief encounter in the gym would've brought out a side to him that made him...well...really attractive. If she hadn't been mistaken, he'd been on the brink of flirting with her. But the part that had shocked her? It was that she had wanted him to.

Flirt! With *her.* The one woman in the whole of Hope Children's Hospital who seemed to rub him up the wrong way just by appearing.

She dug rhe fingernails of one hand into the palm of the other. The woman who liked to keep her own heart as locked away as he seemed to.

Whether she liked it or not, they just might be birds of a feather.

At least it explained the tension.

"Here. Let me help you with that." Finn reached out for the same mat Naomi was lifting and their hands brushed. He pulled his hand back as if she'd branded him with her fingers. She rolled her eyes.

Here we go. Back on familiar territory.

The Mark of The Evil Physiotherapist.

She pulled the mat over to the stack alongside the wall, laid it in place and tried to shake off the grumpy thoughts.

Maybe it was simpler than like attracting like.

Maybe it was a case of a man dealing with his own frailties. Someone as physically capable-looking as Finn—an actual war hero—would not like to be seen as weak, and she'd caught him in an incredibly private moment the other day. Or maybe he'd had an evil physiotherapist back in the day. Not that she was going to ask but physiotherapy wasn't always as fun as it had just been with Ellie. And recovering from an amputation surgery was tough. Just seeing the abject misery on Adao's face brought tears to her eyes.

Finn was a big, strong, physical man. Before his injury she could just imagine how fit he must've been. A young man at the height of his strength and fitness, only to have it taken away by the horror of war. What the man deserved was compassion—not huffs of frustration. It didn't stop her from smarting that he'd rolled back on the flirty behavior he'd shown when Ellie had been in the room. Maybe having her there made it safe. A buffer to ensure nothing would ever really happen.

She knew that feeling. Keeping people at arm's length was her specialty. Except her patients. Her patients *always* went straight to the center of her heart.

"I'm good here if you wanted to get on," she eventually said when all the mats were back in place.

"I was thinking of heading down to the sports center. I owe Charlie a pint after the game the other day."

"Ah." Was she supposed to be inviting herself along or telling him to get a move on?

"You live in town, don't you?"

Was he feeling as awkward as she felt? Because this whole chitchat thing was... Neither of them was really excelling at it.

"Yes."

Why don't you invite yourself along, you idiot? He's clearly trying to ask you if you want to come.

"Would you like to walk into town? Together?" He shifted his weight and kicked up the pace. "And then, of course, I'll go and meet Charlie."

She smiled. It was strangely refreshing to be with someone as awkward at the "making friends" thing as she was.

"Sounds good. I'll just grab my jacket." She jogged across to the small glass office, willing it to magically get curtains or one-way glass so she could bang her head against the wall. *What was she thinking?*

Her heart was pounding against her chest as white noise filled her head.

C'mon, c'mon, c'mon! Behave like a normal human.

It was a walk.

Just a plain old walk. As she stared at her thickly padded winter coat she smiled. Plus point. It was cold enough that they didn't even have to talk if they didn't want to.

Oh, good grief. If they lived at the North Pole maybe. Not Cambridge.

What on earth was she going to talk to Finn Morgan about for twenty whole minutes? How he made her insides turn into an entirely new weather system? How she didn't normally blush when men winked at her? Or how, even if the blush led to something more, he could never follow through because she'd left her heart behind in Africa?

"Everything all right in there?"

"Yeah. Great!" Wow. She didn't know her voice went that high. "'Course. Why?"

"Well…" Finn looked at her through slightly narrowed eyes. "You're just…standing there. Have you lost something?"

My sanity.

"Nope! All good." She pulled on her hoodie and then her puffer jacket over it, yanking the zipper up so fast she nearly caught her chin in it when she hit the top. "Ready to go?"

* * *

Finn was really beginning to question his own grip on reality. What was he *doing*?

First, acting like a first-class show-off idiot in the gym.

Second, asking to walk a girl home like he was a nineteen-fifties teenage boy.

And, third, making up a story about meeting Charlie for a drink when he knew damn well his friend was at home, helping his children decorate the Christmas tree.

What a doofus.

Way to show the pretty girl you like her. Walking mutely along the festively lit streets of Cambridge as if you couldn't wait to shake her off.

Which he couldn't.

He pretended he had to scratch his chin on his shoulder so he could see if she looked as uncomfortable as he felt.

Yup! Pretty much. Romeo of Cambridge strikes again!

Not that he was courting her or anything like that. They were just colleagues, walking down the cobbled streets of a particularly attractive-looking university city on a frosty, clear-skied, festively lit night. Just the type of night that would be perfect for holding one of her mittened hands.

If he liked her that way.

Which he didn't. Not least of all because his dating track record after his ex totaled a handful of one-night stands that never should've happened. Turned out the chicks didn't dig a surly one-legged bastard intent on becoming the best pediatric limb specialist in the UK.

He gave his face a scrub and groaned.

"Oh, my goodness!"

Though she whispered it, Finn heard Naomi's exclamation.

He dropped his hand, hoping she hadn't seen his what-the-hell-am-I-doing-here face. The last thing he needed to introduce into his life was romance. Saying that, he'd be little short of an idiot to ignore the chemistry between the pair of them.

Then again, he was pretty skilled at being an idiot.

What a nightmare.

"Is that...? Is that *Santa*?"

Finn looked to his left and saw Santa appear around a corner. He turned back to Naomi, only to see she was looking the opposite direction…at another Santa.

They and the Santas were just entering Market Square in the city center. The temporary vendors had taken the "deck the halls" edict to the fullest definition. There were long swags of evergreen caught up in bright red velvet ribbons twirled around the lampposts, giving them a North Pole effect. The shopfronts all glittered and twinkled with their own festive displays. The daytime vendors had handed over to the temporary Christmas market stalls that were positively bursting with seasonal delights—edible and otherwise. Someone was roasting actual chestnuts over a crackling fire and from just about every street that led onto the small square was a Santa. And another and another until it finally dawned on them.

"We're in a Santa flash mob!"

They blinked at one another.

Again they'd spoken in tandem. And something about the synchronicity of the moment felt like fairy dust and kismet. Just like the atmosphere in the square. Someone had put on some music and was piping it through speakers Finn couldn't quite locate. Maybe in the vicinity of the huge Christmas tree lit up in a swirl of tiny golden lights.

"C'mon. If we go over here, up onto the church steps, you should be able to see."

"See what?" Naomi jogged a few steps to catch up with him.

"The dancing. I've seen this type of thing on the internet. The Santas all get together, do a dance or sing a carol."

Naomi stopped and blinked her disbelief. "You watch flash mobs on the internet?"

"Moi?" He feigned horror at the thought then shrugged a confessional, "Yeah, maybe..."

Naomi was more than familiar with his roughty-toughty grumble-guts routine. Not that he put it on or anything, she just...there was something about her that spoke to him and somewhere along the way he'd lost his ability to speak back. Growling was a go-to reaction. Overreaction, from the look of things. When she smiled...something he'd seen far too little of...it felt as though his whole world was lighting up from the inside out.

"C'mon." He held his arm out to block the crowds so Naomi could get through and find a good spot to watch as the Santas did, in fact, fall into formation and perform a street dance to a new Christmas song that had whisked its way to the top of the pop charts.

Finn was enjoying watching Naomi every bit as much as he was enjoying the Santas. Her smile was bright and genuine. She clapped along with the crowd when all the Santas encouraged them to do so. She even threw in a few "Woos!" when the dancing elves who'd joined the Santas pulled off a particularly athletic dance sequence. At one point, she dropped her hands after a brisk rub together and one of them shifted against Finn's. Her eyes sped to his as if she'd felt the exact same thing he had when they'd touched. Fireworks.

Naomi was grateful to have found mittens in her pocket for a number of reasons.

One. It was freezing.

Two. They gave her something to fiddle with when Finn looked at her so intently she thought those gray eyes of his were going to bore a hole straight through her and see the myriad sensations that went off in her head when their hands had brushed.

And, three...

There wasn't really a three, other than they were a similar shade of gray to Finn's eyes, which she could not stop staring into, so she needed to make her excuses and go.

"I'm really sorry, I need to—"

"I suppose Charlie's probably waiting for me at the—"

They stared at one another for a moment, their breath coming out in little white puffs, the music and excitement of the flash mob buzzing around them like a blur of fireflies.

"Neither of us are particularly good at finishing sentences tonight," Finn finally said. He tipped his head toward the opposite end of the square but didn't explain why.

"No." Naomi's lips remained frozen in the "O" they'd formed as she looked up at him.

It would be so easy to close that small gap between them. If she just rose up on to the tips of her nearly frozen toes…

"I guess you'd better get to your meeting," she said.

"What?"

Yeah. What? You were having a moment.

"With Charlie? Aren't you meeting Charlie for a drink?" she reminded him.

What are you *doing*? The man was obviously trying to get to know her. He probably just needed a friend. It would be mean to shut him down. Especially since she could do with someone to talk to as well. Someone who understood the types of feelings patients like Adao elicited.

Guilt.

Fear.

Bone-deep sorrow.

Finn shoved his hands in his pockets and cleared his throat. "Yes. Absolutely right. Charlie's probably on his second pint by now." He flicked his hand toward the dispersing Santas. "Easily distracted tonight."

His gray eyes returned to hers, his look so intense she blinked and had to look away.

"Right, well. Thanks for the escort. I mean… company walking back."

"You're all right to get to your flat on your own?"

She looked at Finn as if he'd grown wings and popped on a halo. What was he doing? Going for boy scout of the year to make up for being such a grouch the other day? Or was he actually a genuinely nice guy outside the hospital walls? Maybe he was a bit like her. Wore a mask to work and took it off once he was alone. Only they seemed to have chosen opposite masks to cope. He'd looked so content, so happy with the children at the sports center and even now there were glimmers of that guy standing right in front of her, waiting for her to say something. Do something.

She simply didn't know how to access the "old" Naomi. The one who had never once imagined a world without her parents or boyfriend in it.

"I'm fine." She gave him a tight smile and a little wave and left before they drew out what was quickly becoming a shambles of a farewell.

It wasn't until she'd run up the stairs to her flat, opened the door, thrown her keys into the bowl on the table by the door, just as she'd done every night ever since the hospital had opened, and flicked on the light that she realized she wasn't fine at all.

She had been thrown off balance.

By the unexpected fun of the flash mob.

The impending session she was going to hold with Adao, who still had to crack a smile.

But most of all by Finn.

It had been a long time since someone had unnerved her in this way. And she wasn't entirely sure which way she was hoping it would go.

CHAPTER SEVEN

"DON'T WORRY, ADAO. It's still early days."
Naomi rubbed her hand across the little boy's
shorn head and tried to coax a smile out of his
somber little face.

She'd been giving him a massage and manip-
ulating his shoulder joints to try and prevent
any blood clots. This type of physiotherapy
was critical at this phase of his recovery. And
painful, too.

Adao dropped his head and it all but broke
Naomi's heart to see two fat tears fall onto his
blanket.

"I want Mama and Baaba." Adao's voice
caught on the final word and he barely managed to stem a sob.

Naomi ached to pull him into her arms. Tell
him everything would be all right. His loneliness and grief tore at her chest with a ferocity
she hadn't felt in years.

She wanted her mother and father, too. Not a

single day had passed since they'd been stolen away that she hadn't ached for their presence in her life. And that of her boyfriend. All lost to a foolish war that had, ultimately, come to nothing. Her country was run by the military now. It was a place she'd never be able to call home again.

"I know, love. I know." She gave his head a soft caress and before she could think better of it dropped a kiss on top of his head and pulled him to her for a half-hug, doing her best not to put any pressure on his loosely bandaged wound.

"Hey!"

They both looked up as Finn appeared at the doorway. His hair looked like he'd just come in from a windstorm and his eyes were bright with energy. He gave the doorframe a couple of polite knocks after he'd quickly taken in the scene. "Mind if I come in?"

Adao didn't even bother to disguise the tears now pouring down his gorgeous plump cheeks.

Finn's eyebrows instantly drew together and he crossed the room in three quick long-legged strides. "Are you in pain, little man?"

Adao shook his head. Then nodded. Then

shrugged as the tears continued to fall. It was all Naomi could do not to burst into tears herself.

Physio was often difficult. Often produced tears. Tears of frustration. Tears of pride on a good day, but this was different.

He was a lonely, lost, terrified little boy who wanted his parents.

"Naomi's not been putting you through her torture chamber, has she, mate?"

A few days ago Naomi would've taken umbrage at the question, but now, having seen a new side of Finn, she took it for what it was. A playful attempt to draw a smile from a frightened child. To be honest, she was grateful for the intervention as she was struggling to find anything to say that would make him feel better.

Finn pulled a chair up alongside Adao's bed across from Naomi. He held out his hand for Adao's. When Adao didn't move his, Finn took it in both of his own, ducking his head so he could catch the little boy's eyes.

"Listen, bud. I know this is tough. You know I know, right?"

Adao nodded.

"I showed you mine…and pretty soon you'll be able to show me yours."

"But…all I have is…is…" Adao whispered, tears falling everywhere as he turned to look at his heavily bandaged shoulder. He was still a good week—maybe even a fortnight—away from trying out a prosthesis.

"I know." Finn shot a quick look at Naomi, who pulled a fresh packet of tissues out of her pocket and put them in Adao's lap, keeping one for herself. Just in case.

Definitely, more like. She was already scanning her brain for a private corner just as soon as was humanly possible.

"Bud, look at me. You're talking to someone who's been there and has come out on the other side. The good side. You've got a while yet with the compression garments. They'll support your arm—"

Adao let out a small whimper and then began to cry in earnest.

Just then one of the local hospital volunteers—a lovely grandmotherly type called Mabel—came in with a cup of steaming tea cradled in her hands. She'd assigned herself the task of reading Adao stories since the charity that had brought him here was unable to provide "on the ground" support.

"Oh, Adao!" She threw a quick inquisitive look at Naomi and nodded at the spot where she stood. Obviously it was "her" spot. "Do you mind? I think maybe we need a bit of quiet time."

A swarm of responses jammed in Naomi's throat. All of them were a muddled ache to help and the conflicting, urgent need to push everything back into place that this moment was unzipping.

"Of course." She stepped away from the bed. There was no point in telling Adao she'd be back the next morning. And the next. He was leaning into Mabel's arms and giving himself over entirely to his grief.

Finn took up Adao's charts and quietly explained to Mabel about when to call the nurses for pain management or, if things took a turn for the worse, when to call him.

Naomi felt invisible. Worse, actually. She felt powerless.

Just as she had on *that* day nearly fifteen years ago when her heart had pounded so loudly she could barely hear the shouts and screams. Shame washed over her as the memories slammed to the fore. Her hiding place. The gunfire. The stench of hot metal filling her nostrils as she'd clenched her eyes tight against what she'd known was happening.

Everyone she loved had gone when she'd found the courage to open them again. Fear had turned her into a coward—not a hero like Finn. And with that knowledge came another bitter home truth. She did not deserve unconditional love. She'd thought she'd loved her parents and boyfriend unconditionally, but she had failed at the first hurdle and had just saved herself. And for that solitary selfish act, she could never forgive herself.

"Naomi! Wait." Finn jogged to catch up to her. Damn, she could crank up the speed when she wanted to. No doubt all that running she did along the river.

Not that he'd clocked her doing her stretches outside the hospital most days before shift. No…he didn't do things like that. The less you knew about someone, the easier it was not to care.

And yet here he was, actively avoiding his

own advice. Maybe Christmas was a time of miracles.

"Let me take you to lunch."

Her eyes went wide. He fought not to do the same. He didn't ask women to lunch.

Colleague.

A colleague wrestling with the age-old dilemma. Getting too close to a patient. Most of the time the essential emotional distance needed just clicked into place. It didn't take a brain surgeon—or someone who'd been forced to go through a shedload of PTSD counseling as he had—to see this little boy had wormed his way straight into her heart. And he knew he wasn't the only one to have noticed.

"I've already had a sandwich, thanks." Her tone was apologetic rather than dismissive. And if he wasn't mistaken, the swipe at her eyes wasn't a bit of primping. She was fighting tears.

"Coffee, then." He steered her toward the elevators and put on his best stab at a jaunty salesman's voice. "I hear they've got some festive pastries down in the atrium café. I could grab some and meet you down by the river."

"What?" she snapped, dark eyes flashing

with a sudden flare of indignation. "So you don't have to be seen being nice to me in public?"

"Hey." He lifted his hands up in protest. Talk about wrong end of the stick!

She carried on over him, clearly having found her voice again. A very cross voice. "There's no need. I'm more than happy to carry on working. Unless you think I'm not up to the job." She squared herself off to him, eyes blazing with challenge.

"You're crossing a line." He cut her off cold, the smile dropping from his face. He knew she was upset, but he'd never questioned her professional skills. "No one's doubting your ability to do your job."

She harrumphed. "Are you sure about that? This little talk of yours isn't actually some sugar-laced ploy to let me down easily? Tell me you've decided to put someone else on the case?"

"I will if you carry on like this." Finn meant it, too. There was more than an impassioned plea to do her job crackling in her eyes. Adao's presence here had turned her normally chirpy demeanor raw with emotion.

"Are you *kidding* me?" For a moment Naomi struggled to come up with the best retaliation. "This is what I *do*. It's *all* I do. No hidden talents here. No secret skills in the kitchen. Or special volunteering projects. Sorry to disappoint, *Mr.* Morgan."

"Finn," he corrected her, trying to shake the defensive reaction that shot his shoulders up and around his ears. "And let's leave the sports center out of it, shall we? Those kids are…"

They meant the world to him. Reminded him he had a heart.

"What I do there is different. There's no need to try and rack up bonus karma points to prove you're good at your job. You already are."

She wheeled on him as the elevator doors opened then closed. "You mean you can act like an actual living breathing human being with them but not with me? Fine. Suits me. Once these elevator doors open feel free to take it in whichever direction you like— except *mine*."

Where the hell had that come from? He'd only been trying, in his usual clumsy way, to… Wait a minute. This was all-too-familiar terrain.

Defensiveness. Evasion. Flare-ups followed by pushing the ones you cared about away while deep inside all you really wanted was to be pulled into a deep, reassuring hug and told everything would be okay because you were in a place so dark it was impossible to believe in anything good ever happening again.

She was at war with something that lived deep within her.

Had he become her "someone" she could rail against? The one she was testing?

Despite the fact her entire body was radiating fury, Finn didn't move. He knew how lonely it felt when a person finally succeeded in pushing everyone who cared about them away.

Damn. He cared.

Despite the twitches to fall back into old habits, he held his ground.

His patience paid dividends.

As quickly as Naomi's temper had detonated, a few moments of "I'm not going anywhere" eyes from Finn saw the remaining sparks fizzle and all but disappear. She dropped her head into her hands and huffed out a full-bodied exhalation. After a deep breath in, she let them fall.

"Sorry. I—I didn't mean…" She floundered, trying to find the right words.

His heart softened another notch. Flare-ups were inevitable when the stakes were so high. And there was no doubt about it. Something about Adao had got right under her skin.

Just the same as she had slid right under his.

Two lost souls doing their best to make the world a better place. Sometimes they did good. And sometimes they made a hash of things. Sometimes they did both at the same time.

"C'mon," he said. "Coffee." He punched the elevator button again before tipping her chin up so she was looking him straight in the eye. "And a festive pastry. Doctor's orders."

He turned back to the elevator, trying to disguise his pleasure at eliciting a smile from her. A small one. But it was a smile, nevertheless.

Naomi was one part mortified to one part mollified.

Thank goodness they were outside, walking along the river where there were all sorts of other things and people to look at besides the tall, dark-haired, increasingly intriguing doctor she'd just verbally flayed.

Whoops.

Having a meltdown in front of someone—especially a surgeon—wasn't really her style. Particularly as it hadn't even been about something to do with a patient. This was a hundred percent personal and he knew it. He hadn't rubbed it in, though. For someone whose forte wasn't "cuddly bear"—at least at the hospital—it touched her to see that kind heart she knew he buried under his bluff and bluster rise to the surface.

She blew on her latte before taking a sip of the cinnamon-and-nutmeg-sprinkled drink, sighing as the warm liquid slid down her throat.

"Hit the spot?" Finn asked.

"Yes. And thank you. I'm really sorry—"

"Uh-uh." Finn tutted. "You've already apologized seven times. That's my limit." He stopped and pointed off the path toward a wooden bench made of green sleepers nestled in a sun-dappled copse of silver birches. "This is a good spot."

"You know all the good ones?" A feeble joke, but he gave a little laugh nonetheless. Generous, considering she'd not been showing her best face for the past half-hour. A rare slip.

He gave a vague wave along the towpath. "I live a bit further down the river, so I do actually know all the good spots."

"You live on the river?"

"Literally." He grinned. "Houseboat."

"A houseboat?" She didn't even try to hide her shock. "You."

"Yup. My family moved a lot when I was a kid—military—and I guess life on the move suited me."

"A houseboat?" Naomi couldn't even begin to picture it. Finn was so tall and powerfully built and…well…it was easier to picture him striding across the sprawling slate floors of a huge stone castle than a houseboat.

Finn laughed a full, rich guffaw. "What? You don't think little old me could fit on a houseboat?" He gave her a quick scan then dropped his volume a notch. "You'd be surprised what I can do when I set my mind to it."

Naomi flushed and looked away. Courtesy of Finn Morgan, she'd been surprised quite a few times recently. She had little doubt he could achieve whatever he wanted when he put his mind to it. He'd already pulled at the seams of her perfectly constructed life and exposed her weak spots. No one had done that since she'd arrived in the UK. Not even the emergency refugee staff who'd seen her at her shell-shocked worst when she'd arrived from Zemara. It was as if from the moment she'd arrived she'd had to prove she was worth even the tiniest kindness.

Her foster mother, Charlotte Collins, had been the only one in those early days who she'd felt hadn't been judging her. Her compassion and support had meant so much to her it was why Naomi had legally taken her surname. At that point, to survive, she had needed to look forward. And Charlotte had given her the strength to do so.

Which had been why standing by and doing nothing when Adao had been crying had near enough destroyed her. Little wonder she'd gone on the defensive when Finn had followed her out. She'd been braced for all sorts of words to come hurtling at her: coward, failure, weak, worthless.

But he'd not said a single one of them. Instead, he'd shown her patience. Kindness. And now this…a chance to talk without any pressure.

Following his lead, she took a seat on the bench and sat back to take in their surroundings.

The little woodland nook looked as though it had been designed by Hollywood. Frozen beads of water clinging to the silvery bark shone in the watery sunlight. The river quietly susurrated in the distance as joggers wove their way around couples—old and young—walking alongside the river's towpath. A hoar frost had coated everything overnight and it had yet to melt. Even though the sky was a clear blue today, it was cold and everyone was wearing hats with fuzzy bobbles or silly Christmas jumpers. Or both. No doubt about it. There was a festive buzz in the air. So different from the chaos swirling away in her chest.

"He got to you." Finn's voice was warm. Kind. "Sometimes that happens."

He fell silent, clearly waiting for her to fill in the blanks. Explain why Adao in particular had rattled her otherwise happy-go-lucky cage.

She couldn't go down that path. Not when it already felt as if she was being sucked into a black hole that would lead her straight back to that horrible day when her entire life had changed forever. A hit of iron-rich earth and palm fronds filled her nostrils so powerfully she bit the inside of her cheek and drew blood.

After a few minutes of sitting in silence, Finn, no stranger to keeping himself to himself, realized he wasn't going to get her life story. He hitched his good knee up on the bench and propped his arm on the back of the bench, chin in hand, so he was facing her.

"Next time you need to lash out at someone, maybe you can leave my baking skills out of it? I don't want that secret getting out onto the hospital's gossip train, otherwise the entire surgical staff will be demanding marshmallows like clockwork."

His comically stern expression teased a smile out of her. The second since she'd lost the plot.

How embarrassing to have just snapped like that. And in front of *Finn*, of all people.

"I'm really sorry—" She stopped herself. "I've never done that before."

"It's okay. Better in front of me than in front of Adao, right? And look." He reached out and laid his hand on her arm. "Like I said, it happens."

She stared at his hand, wondering how such

a simple touch could have such a powerful effect on her. Just a colleague giving another colleague a bit of kindness.

But this was Finn Morgan they were talking about. Resident grumpy bear and...well...she was seeing all sorts of differing hues in his "rainbow" these days. In fact, he *had* a rainbow...not just a set of crackling thunderclouds!

She stared out toward the towpath and tried to collect her thoughts. What he'd said was true. It was impossible to be completely neutral at all times. After all, he'd cleared the entire viewing gallery during Adao's operation. Even so, she wasn't feeling particularly proud of herself right now and being on the receiving end of his surprisingly gentle touch was disconcerting. She shrugged her arm away from his hand, disguising the move as a need to give her arms a brisk double rub.

"Cold?"

"No. I mean yes." She rolled her eyes. "I'm always cold here."

"Cambridge or the UK?"

"Both." She frantically thought of a way to nip the direction this conversation was heading in the bud. "But I have an affection for thermalwear so, really, living here suits me to a T!"

Thermalwear? What are you talking about?

Finn didn't press. Either he was completely repulsed by the idea of her in woolen underwear or...oh, no. Was he thinking of her in her underwear? Worst conversation dodge ever.

"So...how do you deal with it?" Naomi tucked her hands into her pockets.

"What? Not let my heartstrings get yanked out of my chest each time I deal with an emotional patient?"

He wasn't patronizing her. He was stating a bald reality of being in the medical profession. Emotions were high. Keeping one's cool was essential. They were health care providers, not family.

"Tell me. What's the 'Morgan Technique'?" She genuinely wanted to know. For the first time in her professional life it seemed impossible.

He didn't even pause to think. "Easy. I think of my dad."

Naomi's heart squeezed tight at the faraway look in Finn's eyes. He didn't elaborate, but he didn't have to. It was enough to hear the warmth in his voice to know he loved him.

Her dad was the reason she'd pushed herself so hard when she'd moved to the UK. "Me too."

The admission was out before she thought better of it. What an idiot. Saying something like that only invited more questions.

"Mr. Collins?" Finn asked. Inevitably. "Was he a physio as well?"

Naomi shook her head. "And Collins wasn't his name."

Why do you keep telling him private things?

"Wasn't?" Finn asked quietly.

Yes. Past tense. She was the only surviving member of her family.

She ignored the question and instead said the family name she'd not spoken in over a dozen years. "Chukwumerije."

"That was your original surname?"

Yes. It had been.

"A tough one for the British tongue to force into submission," she said, doing her best to keep her tone light. She put on an English accent and mangled her name a few times. Finn's laugh echoed throughout the little clearing. He had little crinkles by his eyes. She'd never noticed those before.

An intense need to tell him the whole story took the laughter from her voice.

"There was actually a woman. A lovely woman. Charlotte Collins. She was my foster mother when I came here. Without her..." Naomi's voice cracked and she pressed her fist to her lips to stem a sob of gratitude.

Finn nodded. He got it. She didn't need to spell out just how important compassion was. Kindness.

"Say it again," he asked gently. "Your Zemarian surname."

It was strange, feeling the taste of her own name on her tongue.

For years using the new name had felt like the worst kind of betrayal and also the most generous of blessings.

She'd been granted a new life. A chance to become everything she'd ever dreamed of. But it had only come to pass because of the deaths of those she'd loved most.

Now? Here with Finn? The name felt like a disguise. All part of the chirpy, got-it-together facade she wore day in, day out to keep the demons at bay.

Finn had been mulling over her name. He gave a few aborted starts on mimicking her pronunciation before miming throwing in the towel.

She laughed softly. "When my mother said it, it sounded like poetry. Stella Chukwumerije. She used to say it as if she were royalty."

He raised his eyebrows. The question in his eyes asked one thing and one thing only: Where were they now?

The fact she'd probably never know haunted her dreams every single night.

"My mum's name means star, so sometimes..." She let the rest of the thought remain unsaid as her gaze lifted upwards. Looking up at the stars and believing that maybe, just maybe, her mother was looking down at her offered her solace. Most of the time.

At least Adao's family was alive and well.

An idea sparked. "What if we went onto the internet? Or asked the charity if they have a picture of his parents—maybe them all together as a family. We could put it in a frame for him. I could run and get something from the charity shops now."

Finn smiled as if she'd just handed him a present. "That's a great idea. I'll leave you to the running bit." He pointed at his knee.

"Is it acting up?"

He tipped his head side to side.

The gesture could've meant any number of things.

Yes. No. It always hurts, but I'm a man, so...

"You know—" An offer to give him a massage was just about to fly off the tip of her tongue when he held up a hand.

"I know. I *know.*" Unlike the last time she'd offered help, his defenses didn't fly into place. There might have even been a bit of gratitude in those hard-to-read eyes of his.

In this light they were like sparkling like ice crystals with amber hits of flame...

Oh...

Naomi's body heat shot up a few degrees as their gazes caught and snapped the pair of them into a heightened awareness that blurred everything around them.

Heart. Lungs. Throat. Breasts. Lips. Her *hair*

was aware of Finn. Even more so when he turned toward her on the bench, his knee gently shifting against hers.

It was one of the most sensual feelings she had ever experienced.

Which was ridiculous.

Right?

But it didn't feel ridiculous at all. Not with his face so close she could reach out and trace a finger along the fullness of his lower lip before—

No.

She didn't do this. She didn't *deserve* this. And especially not with a man who came with a complicated past.

His gaze on her own lips was virtually palpable. Her body responded against her will, the tip of her tongue dipping out and licking her lower lip, vividly aware that the only thing separating them was a handful of centimeters and air.

Abruptly, she swiveled so that she was facing the towpath and pressed her knees together.

"It must be nice to have Charlie to confide in after all you've been through."

"What?" Finn shook his head as if not entirely understanding what had broken the spell.

An all-too-familiar deadweight of anxiety began gnawing at that indescribably beautiful ball of heat in her belly and turned it into a churning mass of guilt.

"You know." She heard herself continue, regretting each word as it arrived. "After things changed with your wife."

"*Ex*-wife," Finn bit out, his body language instantly registering the change of mood. "We're divorced."

A cold wind blew in off the river, grazing the surface of her cheeks. A welcome sensation as they were burning with embarrassment.

Finn pushed himself off the bench, his good leg all but launching him toward the towpath.

She remained glued to the bench, in shock at her own—what was it? Stupidity? Common sense?

No. It was worse than that. It was fear. Fear of allowing herself to feel true happiness.

"I'm heading back. Going to do a quick check on Adao before I go into surgery for the rest of the afternoon."

He didn't ask her if she was going to join

him, but he didn't power ahead as she'd imagined he might.

Silently they headed back to the hospital.

"Aren't you going in?" Amanda flicked her head in Finn's direction as he went into Adao's room.

Naomi shook her head. She was more off kilter than when she'd left the room half an hour earlier.

Had she and Finn almost kissed?

"He's not been Captain Grumpy again, has he?"

"Finn? No. Not all. He's—"

"Uh-oh... I see the tides might've shifted where Mr. Morgan is concerned."

Naomi gave Amanda her best "are you crazy" look then went to hover at Adao's doorway, where Finn was talking with Mabel.

"Absolutely we do, Finn. What a lovely idea. I'll just send a little message through on this thingamajig here and see if they can't do it today." The gray-haired woman pulled a mobile phone out of her cardigan pocket and held it out to him, clearly having no intention of sending the message herself.

Finn gave Naomi a quick nod where she was hovering in the doorway. "You still up for getting Adao a frame?" He looked at the little boy whose tears had now dried. "Would you like that, pal?"

Adao nodded, his tear-laced eyes wide with anticipation.

"Right. I guess we'd better send the office a message."

She watched as he made a show of trying to get the tiny phone to obey his large fingers, even managing to draw out giggles from both Adao and Mabel.

When he was done, he handed the phone back to Mabel then chatted a bit more with Adao. Told him how he was still toying with the idea of becoming an astronaut one day. Pointed out what fun going through airport security was now that he had an "iron" leg. Told Adao how lucky he was they were both lefties. Some of the best people he knew were lefties, he said with a wink, before turning to give her a meaningful look.

She was a leftie.

Was there anything the man didn't notice?

Finn was so good with him. It was mesmerizing to watch the pair of them as Finn ever so casually noted Adao's heart rate. Blood pressure. A little bit of swelling that had developed around the joint. There were multiple factors to consider in these early days after the surgery. Joint contracture. Pathological scars. Cardiovascular response to what had been, ultimately, a traumatic event. Residual limb pain. Phantom sensation, edema, and the list went on. All of which Finn nimbly checked while keeping up a light-hearted conversation about Adao's favorite British football players.

It turned out Adao didn't have any. His heart lay with the Spanish.

"What?" Finn feigned receiving a dagger to the heart and only just managing to pull it out. "Not *one* British player?"

Adao shrugged and grinned. He liked who he liked.

Standing there, watching the pair of them banter, Naomi felt an acute sense of loss. She could've kissed this man. This gorgeous, warm-hearted bear of a man.

Would it have been a mistake?

Most likely.

She didn't deserve a fairy-tale moment like

that, let alone the promise of the happiness that could follow in its wake. From what little she knew about Finn, and the stony silence he'd maintained as they'd walked back to the hospital from the river, he wasn't exactly in the market for love. Neither was she, for that matter.

Lust. That's what it had been. A hit of seasonal lust that had taken them both by surprise.

That he was able to treat her as if absolutely nothing had happened between them was proof he compartmentalized his life. Just as she did.

Work.

The sports center for him. The riverside runs for her.

Home.

She tipped her head to the side and scrunched her eyes tight, trying to imagine him in a houseboat, and came up with nothing. The first thing that popped into her mind was a huge man cave carved into the side of a soaring mountainside. Accessible only by foot. Or yak. She easily pictured it all decked out in shaggy woolly mammoth hides and zebra skins. Did it make sense? No. But then again… A huge fire would be roaring in the center of it, with Finn presiding over the place as if he were the king of the jungle. Or the mountain range?

"What's got you so smiley?"

"What?" Naomi shook her head, startled to find both Finn and Adao looking at her as if she'd lost her marbles.

Oh, crikey. She'd gone all daydreamy right in front of the man she was meant to not be daydreaming about.

"Nothing. Just thinking about..." Her eyes darted across the ward to where a Christmas tree was merrily blinking away "I was just thinking about the Christmas party and how much fun it will be."

"Christmas party?" Adao spoke the words as if he'd not let himself imagine such a delight.

Naomi grinned.

"Absolutely." Evie was really outdoing herself if the rumor mill was anything to go by. "It's in a couple of weeks, I think. And..." she held up two sets of crossed fingers "...if everything goes well with your recovery and we get your physio under way, I don't see any reason why you wouldn't be able to go."

Adao looked to Finn for approval.

Finn smiled and gave the little boy's short

head of hair a scrub with one of his huge man hands. "You heard the lady, mate. You focus on getting better and in a couple of weeks' time you might be showing Santa your new prosthesis."

For the first time the mention of the false arm elicited a smile from Adao. "I would very much like to shake Santa's hand," he said.

"Well, then." Naomi's heart was buoyed at the fierce determination lighting up the little boy's eyes. "That's what we shall focus on."

Her gaze shifted to Finn, whose eyes were already on her, his expression unreadable. What had she expected? Him to be all doe-eyed? Hardly. She'd turned him down. He was getting on with his life as if it had never happened and what lay deep in those moonstone-colored eyes of his would remain a mystery. No matter how much curiosity was getting the better of her.

She gave Adao a quick wave goodbye and headed toward the stairwell, fighting the growing sensation that running away from Finn could be one of her biggest mistakes to date.

CHAPTER EIGHT

AN EMPTY GYM.

No music.

Just the pounding of his heart and the sound of his breath.

The best part about an exhausting workout was that there was no room in Finn's head for anything other than the weights in his hands and the resistance his body was or wasn't giving as he pushed himself to the next level.

There wasn't one spare second to consider just how close he'd come to kissing Naomi the other day.

Or if he'd been counting: six days, twelve hours and a handful of minutes ago.

But he hadn't been counting.

Or popping round when she was giving Adao one of his physio sessions, taking careful note of how gentle she was with him. Sensitive to how lonely and lost the boy was feeling.

Neither had he been so much as giving the

slightest thought to those beautiful, full lips of hers. The slight tilt of her eyes rimmed by lashes so thick and long he could almost imagine them butterfly-kissing his cheek.

Almost.

But he wasn't thinking about things like that.

He wasn't letting himself notice that when she walked into a room the world felt a little bit nicer.

Or the soft curve of her neck.

How watching her work with patients was seeing someone answering a calling, not doing a job.

Or the gentle swoops and soft curves her body revealed even in the athletic gear she almost always wore to work.

Finn strode over to a press-up bench and took off his prosthesis. A challenge. That's what he needed. He dropped to the floor and did a few press-ups, unsuccessfully trying to rid his brain of that instant—that bit of other-worldly time and place—when he'd been absolutely sure they'd both moved toward the other.

Two lost souls finding solace in each other.

Only he had no idea if she really was a lost

soul or not. Something about Adao had well and truly shot her emotions up to explosive level. Then again, he never saw her raise her voice or offer anything less than a smile to every other member of staff.

Maybe it was him. Maybe it was the combination of the pair of them. Maybe it was the fact he'd never come to terms with pushing his ex-wife so hard the only choice she'd had in the end had been to leave him.

"Mr. Morgan!" The door to the gym was pushed open and Theo appeared. He was dressed in running gear. In his usual swift, efficient manner he took in a sweaty senior surgeon, a discarded prosthesis, a look that could kill and said, "Want a spotter?"

No. He wanted to be left alone to wallow in his misery. Only…he didn't really.

Blimey. Since when did misery *actually* love company?

Theo crossed to the press-up bench and eyed the weights Finn had loaded on the bar. He clearly knew better than to wait for an invitation.

"Looks like you're weighted light tonight."

Theo had the world's best poker face and he

was playing it hard right now. He knew Finn only pressed weights that challenged him at the highest level.

"I could lift this with my pinky," Finn grunted, not even caring that Theo was his boss. Not right now anyway.

"Well, then. Show me."

Finn craned his neck before lying back on the bench. Rather than address the obvious—his unusual decision to work out stripped back to his true self—he threw a question at Theo. "You look like you could pound out a few frustrations yourself."

Theo sucked in a sharp breath. "That obvious?"

"Only to a seasoned doctor."

Theo huffed out a mirthless laugh. "You mean like all the other doctors we've got wandering round Hope?"

"Something like that." Finn lay back on the bench and wrapped his hands round the bar. "Only…to…the…rest…of…them…you… look…achingly…handsome."

To Finn's relief, Theo took the jibe as it was intended and chuckled. Something to break the tension that had added more than a silver hair or two to Theo's temples.

Ivy wasn't getting any better. Quite the opposite, in fact. No amount of testing, Doodle visits or letters to Santa Claus were making a blind bit of difference.

Theo's hands floated just under the bar as Finn cranked out three rounds of three lifts before pushing himself up. "You want a go?"

Theo eyed him for a minute as if he were being asked to a duel then did the standard guy response. "Get up, then. You're on my bench."

"Your bench?" Finn guffawed loud and hard then made a show of wiping it clean and presenting it as if it were a throne. "Your majesty."

Theo flicked him a look that said, *Enough with the servitude, mate*, then settled on to the bench.

True. It was Theo's bench. His gym. His hospital. But the last thing he'd ever seen the man be was proprietorial or smug about his financial status. Billionaire. What the guy was was a worried dad. And letting off steam had to be hard when your little girl's health was deteriorating right in front of your eyes.

"How's the diagnostician getting on?"

"Madison?" There was a bite in his voice when he said the name and he ripped off three quick rounds, pressing the same weight Finn had.

Impressive.

Or emotion-fueled.

Easy to see there wasn't much point in asking him if Madison had made much progress. His heart went out to Theo, seeing his little girl, the only one left in his family, go through so much pain right in front of him and feeling utterly powerless. It was one of the reasons he'd stripped himself of his own friends and family. No one to lose. Then, of course, there was the flipside…nothing to gain.

"Want to do another round?"

Theo lifted the bar and began pressing again. The determination on his face reminded him of his own once he'd decided to retrain as a pediatric surgeon. He'd poured everything he'd had into becoming the best. Apart from work, he'd barely imagined wanting to properly live again—let alone love again. And while he was nowhere near loving Naomi, he barely knew the girl, he felt more connected to her on a visceral level than he had with anyone.

Maybe it had taken this long for him to figure out who the hell he was. His whole life he'd worked toward becoming a soldier. Then he had been a soldier for five incredible years. Then in one solitary instant everything he'd thought he'd become had been taken away from him.

Why would his wife and family want a fraud?

And then this beautiful, mysterious, happy, sad, talented and obviously conflicted woman had walked into his life and another bomb had gone off.

For the first time in over a decade, taking the risk seemed better than going back down that soul-sucking rabbit hole he'd swan-dived into after his life had changed forever.

Theo clanged the bar back into place, sat up and stared right through Finn.

Um...

"Christmas plans?" Finn asked.

What the—?

King of casual chitchat he was not.

"You're looking at them," Theo said, lying

back down, pressing out one more round then getting up and whirling round on the bench. "This, and trying to find my daughter a Christmas miracle. What about you?" He glared at Finn as if daring him to have better plans.

"Ditto." He opened his wide arms to the gym.

They stared at one another then laughed. "Couple of real players on the social circuit, aren't we?" Theo pushed himself up from the bench, gave it a swipe with the towel he'd grabbed on the way in. "I'm going for a run." His eyes flicked to Finn's good leg. "Want to come?"

"Nah." He had a prosthesis that was great for running, but he wasn't in the mood. He'd come here to test himself. See if he was ready—not just physically—to move away from the past and see how he got on with the future.

Naomi heard the weights drop to the rubberized gym floor before she entered the room. It wasn't unusual for staff to use the large physio gym, but it was definitely rare to hear such heavy weights in use. Aware that being startled could throw whoever was in there off their stride, she slipped into the gym as innocuously as she could.

The sight she saw actually took her breath away.

Finn Morgan.

Bare-chested.

Athletic shorts exposing a leg so toned it would've made Michelangelo gasp.

She pressed her fingers to her lips to stop herself from doing the same.

Finn's body glowed with exertion as, without even wearing his prosthesis, he alternated between single leg barbell lifts and pull-ups.

His back was to her, but she could see his focused expression in the mirrors on the far side of the gym. She'd never seen such a display of precision and resolute determination.

Despite the use of heavy weights, Finn's body wasn't over-pumped, like some of the zealous gym rats she'd seen throughout the years.

No. Finn's tall form had heft, but it was toned to absolute physical perfection. She could see clear definition in his shoulders and biceps as he pulled himself up and over the pull-up bar with the fluid grace of a gymnast. The muscles in his back rippled with the lithe strength of a lion.

Parts of her own body lit up as if she were a freshly decorated Christmas tree. She hadn't felt warm tingles of response below her belly button in just about forever and now Finn seemed to have some sort of remote control on her internal fireworks display—just one solitary glance could detonate an entire evening's worth.

When he dropped to the floor and took a double hop across to where he'd laid the heavily weighted barbell, she watched quietly as his internalized focus manifested itself in an extraordinary show of physical strength and courage. Not every man would put himself to the test like this. Not every man would win.

He'd obviously been working out for a while and when he crouched to pick up the barbell she saw him hesitate before heaving the sagging bar up and over his head. As he held it aloft and looked toward the mirror to monitor his form, his eyes shifted across to her and he threw the weight to the floor with a crash.

"I'm sorry, I didn't mean to interrupt. I was just going to set something up for a patient."

Finn turned to her and said nothing as he reached out an arm to steady himself.

He dipped to the floor and scooped up a white towel and wiped his face.

She'd never seen him without his prosthesis. Well. Not glossed in sweat and half-naked, anyway.

He certainly didn't need it, or anything else to prove that he was anything less than a powerfully driven man.

She'd never wanted to touch someone more in her entire life.

"Do you need these for your next patient?" Finn asked.

"No." Naomi held up her wrist as if her timepiece-free arm would remind him it was well after hours. "I thought I'd just get a head start on tomorrow and set up some equipment for my first appointment."

Neither of them moved.

Tension crackled between the pair of them as if a power line had been torn from its stable housing and set loose in a wind storm. Sparks flying everywhere. No clear place to hide.

"I've got a trick that might help you with your dead lifts."

Finn arced an eyebrow. Go ahead, the gesture read. Improve on perfection if you can.

He wasn't smug. He was just right.

Well. Almost right.

"Your hips. You're not using them as the power thrusters they're designed to be."

Naomi flushed as she spoke. If he were a patient she would normally move up behind them and...well...they would go through the motions together, but...

Her throat tickled. She was suddenly feeling really *parched.*

Her hand moved along the length of her throat as if it would ease the dry, scratchy sensation. A drink of water would be good about now.

As if mirroring her thoughts, Finn dipped to the floor again and grabbed a bottle of water, unscrewed the cap and, eyes still on her, began gulping down the water as if he'd just emerged from the desert.

Her eyes were glued to a solitary trickle of water wending its way through his dark stubble on his throat, shifting along his clavicle, heading toward that little sternal dip between the bones, only to be swiped away by a towel.

She caught Finn's grin as he dropped the towel on a nearby bench and shot her a surreptitious glance. He'd seen her ogling him. And he'd enjoyed it.

"That's a pretty intense workout you have there."

"No excuses," he said.

Wow.

It was that simple.

Of course it would be. For a man who worked with amputees, not to mention his time at the sports center where the wheelchair-bound athletes pushed themselves to achieve more, do better, try again, and never give up, no excuses sounded like a pretty solid motivator. He was making himself an example for his patients.

Only...she wondered if they could see the dark shadows flickering across those eyes of his. The man knew loss. The man knew pain. Whether or not she wanted to admit it, they were kindred spirits. But could two souls who had known devastation create something good?

He hopped over to the press-up bench and strapped on his prosthesis. When he rose again, squaring himself off to her as he pulled on his long-sleeved T-shirt, about a million butterflies took off, teasing her body's erogenous zones as if he were tracing his fingertips along the surface of her skin as his eyes drank her in.

"Well, then." She gave her hands a brisk let's-get-to-it rub. "If you're up for it, let me add some notches to your bow."

Finn stood absolutely still, his eyes cemented to hers. "I don't think that's what you meant to say."

"Of course I—" Naomi stopped. Had she?

Sometimes, even though it had been over ten years, she still muddled up British expressions. Her eyes widened as she realized how the expression could have been taken. Sexually.

"Oh, I didn't—"

Before she could form a coherent thought, Finn crossed to her and she was in his arms, his mouth descending on hers as if the world's most powerful magnets had drawn them together. When he first came up for air he looked into her eyes as if this had been the moment he'd been waiting for. The moment when his life would change forever.

She recognized the fire, because she felt the very same heat incinerating her every intention to remain immune to him. To protect her heart.

Her hands flew to his face, the pads of her fingertips enjoying the contrast between the hot, needy demands of his mouth and the masculine prickle of his stubble.

There was not a single cell in her in body with the power to resist. Neither did she want to.

One of his hands slid round her waist and pulled her tight to him. As if she wasn't already arching into the solid heat of his chest. No one needed to tell them her body had been designed for his.

Finn slid his free hand up the nape of her neck and pulled back for a moment, looked deep into her eyes then changed tack, descending once again, to taste her in slow, luxurious hits of teasing kisses. He threaded his fingers into her loosely woven solitary plait and tipped her head back, dropping heated kiss after kiss on her throat.

Staying silent wasn't an option.

It was the first moan of pleasure she had ever heard roll from her throat.

These were no ordinary kisses. This was no ordinary connection.

Desire. Hunger. Need.

They were slaking all of them, their bodies and mouths moving intuitively as if the universe had aligned its entire history for this very moment.

In the center of her fiercely pounding heart Naomi knew this moment would be forever branded on her soul.

And she also knew it could never happen again.

Not unless she made peace with her past—and fifteen years on it still seemed an impossible task.

Finn sensed the change in Naomi's body language before she pulled away. They were the matching pieces of the puzzle of his life. He knew that in the very marrow of his bones.

When she stepped back, he didn't try to stop her. He couldn't.

His entire body was jacked up on adrenaline and hormones and one single move toward her might betray just how powerfully—how *intimately*—she had touched him. Had touched his heart.

"Don't let me keep you if you need to set up your equipment."

Naomi shook her head as if he were speaking a foreign language.

"No. It's fine. It can wait. I was just being hyper-prepared."

"Avoiding your life, you mean?"

Her expression became shuttered, her eyes protectively dropping to half-mast.

"I do exactly the same thing, Naomi. Take every shift going. Work out here just in case my phone goes. Tell myself, *Look. Someone needs me.* I'm trying to find proof, I suppose." He looked her straight in the eye. "Proof there's a reason why I exist."

She didn't even bother to protest. Didn't need to. He could see it in her eyes. She shared exactly the same fears he had.

A gut-clenching fear that he hadn't done enough to be worthy of the life he had.

It was the most honest he'd been with anyone in years. And every word he'd uttered was nothing less than the plain truth.

Hard to confront. Abrasive even. But *real.*

The door swung open and Evie appeared with an elf's hat on her head and a Christmas wreath dangling from her arm. She was all smiles these days and today was no different. "Hey, you two! Coming upstairs for the carol concert in the foyer? Free mince pies and mulled wine for the over-eighteens who aren't on duty!"

Naomi just stared at her as if she were a ghost.

Mercifully, Evie whirled around with a wave and a merrily trilled "Fa-la-la-la-la" before registering the shock of being interrupted on their faces.

"Carols?" Finn asked, as if it were the natural progression of snogging the woman of your dreams— Wait. *Woman of his dreams?* That was going to take some processing.

Naomi shook her head and pointed vaguely to another part of the hospital. "I've got to check on someone."

No, she didn't.

The message was clear. She was saying something, *anything,* to get as far away from him as possible.

"Fine."

His stiff, abrupt movements as he pulled on his outdoor gym clothes spoke volumes. He didn't want this to end. He wanted it to be the beginning. The frustrated yanks he gave his hoodie as he pulled it over his head and down across his torso—yes, he caught her looking when his shirt hitched up, *ha!*—were all far too familiar reactions for him. He'd behaved the same way with his ex-wife. Pushed her away when the going had got tough.

Well, he wouldn't give Naomi the chance. Not tonight. Not ever.

He pretended not to watch as she went over to the duffel bag she'd brought in and pulled out a bright red picture frame with a tropical theme embossed along the edges. She turned around with a shy smile and showed him what looked like a family photo. "For Adao."

Ah…

She actually was going to see someone.

He pressed his fingers to his eyes and gave his head a good shake. What an idiot.

He raised a hand to wave goodbye, but when he looked toward the doorframe she had already gone.

CHAPTER NINE

PACING ON A houseboat wasn't much of a tension-reliever.

Finn loved the place even though he near enough brained himself on the doorframes every single day. The warm wooden planks. The compact but modern kitchen. The old leather sofa he'd wrangled in through the small rooftop hatch by sheer force of will.

The ability to untie himself from the mooring and set off whenever the mood struck.

It's how he'd ended up here in Cambridge. He'd bought the portable home when his stint at rehab and his marriage had come to mutual and abrupt endings. He'd stayed in the Manchester area for a while to keep up with his rehab. But really? Once he'd cut ties with his past, he'd liked the idea that he could just cast off whenever he wanted and just go.

He stared at the phone for a minute, then picked it up, checking that he still had his ex-wife's number. His mum had sent it to him "just in case." She never nagged, but about once a year she asked if he'd "heard anything on the grapevine."

The way he'd treated Caroline gnawed at his conscience.

They'd not been a match in the end. They'd been kids who'd married too soon, all caught up in the romance of him going off to war. The last thing they'd been equipped for had been for him to come back at the ripe age of twenty-four with one good leg and a seething ball of fury where the other one had been.

He'd been angry with everything and everyone back then. Most of all himself. But his immediate family had taken the brunt of it.

His parents had retired to Spain a while back and, before they'd gone, the three of them had made their peace. They got it.

It wasn't simply the loss of his leg. It was losing the army as well. It was his family's chosen profession. His family's *history*. And for the first time ever…a Morgan was stepping away from the front line.

Sure. It had been bad luck. No one looks to get injured.

But Caroline…bless her…she hadn't been who he'd needed at his darkest hour.

And now, fourteen years after coming out of that pitch-black tunnel, he was beginning to think he'd found the woman he could open his heart to.

Someone who understood a core-deep sense of loss.

When Naomi looked into his eyes she seemed to see all of the trauma he'd endured and more. The pain. The doubt. The urgent, primal need to do better. To *be* better.

All the things he saw when he looked into Naomi's eyes.

She *knew* him.

And for the first time since he'd cleared his social calendar of anything more than a casual fling he wanted more.

He wanted Naomi.

He stopped his pacing and snorted out a laugh as he remembered Theo warning him about wearing through the floorboards at the hospital. To do so on a houseboat would be little short of a disaster. He scanned the cabin, looking for something, anything, to do.

A stack of cookbooks lay front and center on his dinky kitchen island.

When in doubt?

Bake.

And while whatever he'd decided to rustle up was in the oven, he'd call Caroline. It was about fourteen years overdue, but...maybe he'd needed the time.

He began pulling ingredients out of the cupboards.

Excuses. Everything he thought up to say to her was an excuse.

The truth was, he'd met someone.

And if he were going to be in any sort of place to even try having a relationship, he needed to make peace with his past.

A quick look at the ward clock showed it was just after eight.

Naomi had ended up getting wrangled into listening to a few of the carols by a very happy Alice and Marco who'd let it slip they'd set their wedding date for just before Christmas.

She hoped they hadn't noticed her fingers leap to cover her kiss-bruised lips as they'd spoken of their excitement about spending the rest of their lives together.

She'd made her excuses, something easily done in the hospital, and had come up here to see Adao. Chances were he was asleep, but even if she was able to tiptoe into his room and place the framed photo of him with his family near him, it would be nice for him to wake up to.

It wasn't as if she was going to get much sleep tonight.

Kissing like teenagers!

No.

She shook her head.

What had happened with Finn had been two consenting adults ripping open a pent-up attraction. And from the looks of things, neither of them had any idea what to do next.

She'd had a couple of boyfriends, but nothing with this level of passion. If the gossip was anything to go by, Finn was a renowned lone wolf so... He was such a mystery to her and yet...a part of her felt like she'd been waiting her whole life to find him because she'd known him all along.

Those *kisses.*

Fireflies danced around her belly at the thought.

She'd kissed like a teenager with her boyfriend back in Zemara. It had been sweet. Innocent. Two young people focused on school, getting into university and then, when war had broken out, surviving.

She glanced at the photograph she'd managed to get from the medical charity.

In it Adao's face was alight with an ear-to-ear grin. He was holding a puppy in one arm and had his other arm flopped round his big sister's shoulders from his perch atop a large wooden barrel. His parents were behind the pair of them, also smiling. It was a perfect family photo and reminded her so much of how happy she had been with her own family that a prickle of impending tears teased at her throat.

She shook it away as she approached Adao's room. She was here to comfort him, not cry about her own past.

Her eyes shot wide open when she reached the room. Far from asleep, Adao was wide awake, with a huge, cuddly labradoodle sprawled across his lap.

Alana, Doodle's minder, was sitting in a chair a couple of meters away, reading a book.

Naomi tapped on the doorframe.

"Okay if I come in?"

Alana nodded toward Adao. It was up to him.

He looked at Doodle and the dog wagged his tail so he smiled and nodded.

"I've brought you something I thought you might like to put by your bed."

"Really?"

The astonishment in his voice tugged at her heart.

She pulled the photo out from behind her back and showed it to him.

Tears instantly sprang to the little boy's eyes. Naomi held her breath, suddenly worried it was the worst possible thing she could have given him. She hadn't been able to look at any photos of her own family since they had been taken away that horrible day. They existed. In an envelope buried deep in the back of her cupboard. But to look at their smiling, beautiful faces every day and know she'd never see the real things again? She didn't know that she had the strength.

"I love it. I love it so much. Thank you, miss."

"Naomi," she gently corrected.

He repeated her name as if tasting it, his eyes still glued to the photo. He pulled the photo close to his chest and hugged it, then lifted it up to his face and gave each of his family members a kiss.

Out of the corner of her eye Naomi saw Alana reaching for the box of tissues near her chair.

She didn't blame her. The moment was about as powerful as they came. She was struggling to keep her own tears in check.

Adao's face brightened as an idea struck. He showed the photo to Doodle. The dog sat up and listened as Adao pointed out his mother, father and sister. Then listened to a detailed explanation of where the picture had been taken—outside their home—when it had been taken—after they'd come home from church—what they had eaten afterwards—a huge meal with the rest of the members of their congregation—and how he had played and played with his friends that day. Played until the sun had gone down, when all their mothers had called them in and made them go to bed so they would be fresh for the next day at school.

His voice had cracked a bit at the end, but it was the happiest he'd ever sounded.

In fact, it was the most Naomi had ever heard him speak.

From the astonished look on Alana's face, it was the most she had heard as well.

"Good idea," the blonde woman mouthed.

"Naomi?" Adao was holding the photo out to her. "Could you please put this up so Doodle and I can see it from the bed?"

"Of course." She made a bit of a to-do about rearranging the scant items on top of his bed-side table and put the photo front and center as Adao lay back on his pillow. "Is this good here?" She gave it a tiny shift closer toward him.

He looked at Doodle for confirmation. The dog lifted his head and tilted it to the side as if checking it from the same angle as Adao, then gave a little woof.

Adao beamed. "Thank you."

"You're welcome. I'm so pleased you like it."

There was a light knock on the door. Navya, one of the night sisters on the ward, was wearing The Look. It was gentle but firm, and it meant it was time to go now.

Naomi dropped a kiss on Adao's head. "See you tomorrow, okay?"

For the first time he didn't look at her fearfully and a huge warmth wrapped around her heart.

She walked to the elevator with Alana and Doodle, amazed at seeing the change in the little boy.

She gave the dog's head an affectionate rub and smiled. "Does everyone tell him their secrets?"

"A lot of people do. Mostly the children," Alana conceded with a smile. "But you know what they say."

Naomi shook her head and entered the elevator along with the pair of them. "What do they say?"

Alana cocked her head to the side at the same time as Doodle. "A problem shared is a problem halved. Or something like that. Maybe it's burden." She shrugged and grinned. "Better out than in is what it boils down to. Isn't that right, Doodle?" She gave the dog a loving stroke. "This guy knows far too much about me. I'm surprised he doesn't put his paws on his ears and start to howl half the time."

Naomi laughed along with her, but the words were hitting home. She'd never shared her story with anyone. Not even the girls and women she'd first bunked with at the refugee facility she'd stayed in when she'd first moved to the UK. She'd nicknamed the facility "The House of Secrets."

Naomi had convinced herself it was best to keep her story close. Hidden. But between kissing Finn and watching Adao pour out his life story to this adorable pooch…it was like the universe was offering her sign after sign that now was the time she needed to share her story.

And she knew exactly who she wanted to share it with.

The elevator doors opened and Alana and Doodle began to head toward the main exit. "Are you walking to the car park?"

Naomi shook her head. "I think I'm going to take a little walk along the river."

"It's freezing out there. Make sure you wrap up warm."

Naomi watched as the pair ambled out of the hospital and toward the car park then set off with a gentle jog along the riverbank.

She'd know Finn's place when she saw it.

Something told her the universe was working in her favor tonight and it was time to start reading the signs.

Finn was pulling the cake out of the oven when he heard the knock on the door.

What the—?

No one visited him. Ever.

He opened the door, feeling almost as shocked as Naomi looked to see him there.

"I need to tell you something. To explain." She spoke low and urgently, as if she might implode if she didn't get whatever it was she had to say out soon.

"I have one cake, two forks and a bottle of red."

Wow. He was a real Romeo, wasn't he?

Her brows drew together as if he'd just told her he was from the planet Zorg. Her short, quick breaths told him she was running on adrenaline. Maybe he should've offered the standard cup of tea and a biscuit. The rest could wait.

"Come on in."

A few minutes later, coat off, but with a

woolen blanket wrapped round her shoulders, Naomi sat across from him at the small wooden table with a fork in her hand, a cup of steaming tea in front of her—she'd refused the wine—and a cake between them.

"Um… This all right?" Finn gave his dark tangles a scrub. "I don't really do hosting. No one really ever calls round."

"I've never been offered an entire chocolate cake before."

"Guess this is a day of firsts."

They looked at one another, their gazes catching and clasping tight. Of course it was a day of firsts.

First kisses being the most memorable of all.

But she wasn't here to talk about kissing, so he sat back and waited.

The air between them was alive with pent-up energy and yet…somehow it felt right, Naomi being here in his man cave.

"I saw Adao just now."

"The picture? How did that go?"

"He loved it. Alana was there with the therapy dog, Doodle. He told Doodle all about his family. His life…" Her gaze shifted down to her hands where she was rubbing her thumb along the spine of the fork as if trying to re-mold it into an entirely new shape.

Something clicked. He saw where this was going. She wanted him to be her Doodle.

"I'll take the first bite, shall I? Save you the embarrassment."

"Embarrassment?"

"Of wanting to wolf down the entire cake in one go." He took a huge forkful and made a show of really enjoying it. Which, even if he had made it himself, didn't require much acting. Who didn't like warm chocolate cake?

Following his lead as he plunged his fork into the large cake, Naomi took a daintier portion, her eyebrows lifting as she tasted the cake. "Oh, wow! Mmm... This is delicious."

"I've been competitive baking with a television show," he confessed. "So far I think I'm winning."

Naomi put her fork down, her expression sobering. "I need to explain why Adao means so much to me."

"You don't need to explain anything you don't want to."

"I want to." Her gaze locked with his and everything he saw within those dark brown eyes of hers seared straight into his chest cavity. She was a kindred spirit. A fellow lost soul who, if he was strong enough for her, just may have found her mooring.

He pulled his own mug of tea toward him, took a drink, sat back and listened.

"Many years ago…fourteen and a bit…"

He nodded. It was about the same length of time since he'd lost his leg.

She stopped, drummed the table with her fingers then backtracked. "When I was seventeen, my country was disrupted by civil war. Up until then I had lived a happy childhood. Just like anyone else. Maybe just like you."

Finn nodded as confirmation. He'd had a great childhood. Military through and through. Moving every few years. New countries. New parts of the UK. Always "on mission" to make himself the best possible candidate for army recruitment when the time came…

"It all changed so quickly. One day my boyfriend and I were going to school like normal teenagers—"

"Your boyfriend?" Finn prompted. There was no point in editing her story on his account.

She gave him a weak smile. "It was a teen-age romance."

"Hey." Finn raised his hands. "I'm not going green-eyed monster on you. Everyone has a past. I have mine. You have yours." He laid his hands on top of hers and gave them a light squeeze. "The only thing I am here to do is listen."

And learn. And something told him right then and there he'd stay and be there for her as long as it took. Everyone had a past. And everyone had a future. It took moving on from one to get to the other, and that was precisely what he was hoping to do.

CHAPTER TEN

NAOMI SEARCHED FINN'S intense expression for any fault lines.

Not a single one.

Just a solid, warm-hearted, generous man sitting across from her with nothing other than her own well-being in mind.

It was painful. But she began to speak.

"For the most part, the rebels hadn't been around our small town. It was about the size of Cambridge, actually. It had a river. And a hospital." She suddenly became lost in memories of just how much she had taken for granted before the war had begun. A quiet, bustling market town where her father had run a hardware store and her mother had been a teacher. She'd always had food. Clothes. They'd had a happy, perfectly normal life.

"Had you always wanted to be a physiotherapist?" Finn asked, dipping his fork into the cake and indicating she should feel free to help herself.

She smiled but shook her head. She couldn't eat cake and tell this particular story. "I knew I always wanted to help people, but I wasn't sure how. I used to volunteer at the hospital as... I'm not sure what you call them here. In Zemara we had a lot of American missionaries, so we were called candy-stripers. We worked in pinstripe pinafores to identify us as volunteers. It was good fun. I loved it whenever I could help a patient smile or laugh."

"I bet you were great at it."

Her smile faded. "I had only done it for about a year, but it was long enough to discover physiotherapy. I really enjoyed seeing the rehabilitation side of working with patients."

"Sometimes that's the hardest part."

"Exactly!" She felt the original spark of passion for the job still burning bright within her. "That's what drew me to it. The challenge of instilling a sense of pride in the patient. Changing the parameters. Looking at things from a new perspective."

"That's how it works all right." Finn put his fork down and took a gulp of tea. "There were about a thousand times I wished I could've unscrewed my head from this old lunky body of mine and screwed a different one on it."

She gave him a sidelong look. From where she was sitting he was looking pretty close to perfect.

"One with a positive attitude," he explained.

Ah. Well. "Everyone has their down days." She took a sip of her tea and lifted her gaze to meet Finn's. He really was an extraordinary man. A flush crept to her cheeks but she ploughed ahead and said what she was thinking. "For what it's worth? I'm glad you kept the one you had."

They looked at one another in the soft light and if Naomi hadn't come here for another reason entirely she would've been hard pressed not to lean across the table and start kissing him all over again.

Though she'd seen his fiery side, she knew now his temper was usually directed at himself. He was fiercely loyal. That was much apparent. And brave. Her thoughts skipped to Charlie and the look of true respect and admiration he'd given Finn when telling Naomi how Finn had saved his life.

She hadn't saved anyone's life.

And therein lay the crux of the matter.

He was a hero. She was a coward. No wonder she was drawn to him.

She played with her fork for a minute. Took a sip of her tea. She wasn't here to talk about physio. Or her childhood. She was here to explain to Finn why she'd become so emotional about Adao. Too much emotion fueling too many memories.

"The rebels came when we were least expecting it."

Finn nodded, showing no sign of being surprised they'd changed from talking about his head to her home town being invaded by armed rebels.

"I was down at the river, seeing if there had been a catch that day. Food had been…scarce in the previous weeks. We weren't starving but the country had slowly been falling under their reign of terror."

A shiver juddered down her spine at the memory of the helicopters flying overhead, the wild-eyed recruits practically hanging out of the open doors and firing their machine guns indiscriminately. Men, women, children. They hadn't cared. Most of the rebels' so-called cavalry had been poor men bribed with alcohol and drugs. Men who, in another world, could have been convinced to turn their energies to doing good had they been offered food and shelter instead. She tugged the edges of the soft cashmere blanket Finn had draped round her shoulders closer together.

"C'mere." Finn rose and gestured to the comfortable-looking sofa. Worn, golden leather. When she sank into a corner and pulled a cushion onto her lap she felt protected, safe. Finn threw a couple of logs into a small wood burner she hadn't noticed earlier. An image of Finn chopping the precisely cut woodpile by hand flickered through her mind before his silence reminded her she needed to get through this story.

"I heard the helicopters first. My instinct was to run home. I'd asked my boyfriend to meet me there so that we could all eat together that night, but when I heard the shooting and screaming... I..." She pressed her hands to her ears, still hearing the cries of disbelief and fear coming from the normally tranquil country town. "I hid." The words came out as a sob.

"I hid underneath some palm leaves I found drying at the edge of the forest because I could see from there. They were loading everyone they could into trucks. Men in some. Women and children in others. They were screaming at everyone to hurry. Telling lies. Saying that they were taking them to refugee camps where they would be safe, but everybody knew where they were really going."

"The mountains?" Finn asked softly.

She nodded, swiping at the tears cascading down her cheeks. From the grim look on his face he knew exactly what a trip to the mountains would have meant for her family and the rest of those other poor, innocent people. The excavation of the mass graves that had been found there only warranted one or two lines of mention in the newspapers these days, but Naomi lived with the knowledge that those she had loved most dearly were very likely amongst the bodies slowly being recovered.

Finn handed her a handkerchief from his pocket. "It's clean."

Their fingers brushed as she accepted the cotton square and the hit of connection felt like a lifeline. A chance to believe in the possibility that one day the weight of guilt might not be as heavy as it was at this very moment.

She swiped at her tears and when she'd steadied her breath she finished her story as quickly as she could. "I hid under the palms for three days."

His eyes widened. "What about food? Water?"

She shook her head. "I was too terrified to move. It rained at night anyway…a warm rain…so I drank what I could from the palm fronds. Even if there had been food I am sure I would have not been able to eat it." Her hands balled into two tight fists in front of the cushion she'd been hugging. "My stomach was tied in knots that day. Permanent knots of guilt and sorrow and shame that I did nothing to help my family."

"Do you still feel that way?"

Pain lanced through her heart. "Of *course* I do. They're still gone. I know the chances of them ever reappearing are minimal. No. They're not even that." She scrubbed her hands through her hair and looked Finn directly in the eye. "They will never come back. And I will have to live with that guilt for the rest of my life."

"Guilt for what? You wouldn't have been able to save them. If anything, you would've been killed trying or..."

He didn't finish his sentence. He didn't have to. If she'd run and joined her mother on the truck, she would have died with her. But what was the point in living if everyone you loved died knowing you did nothing?

"Have you spoken to anyone else about this? There are professionals who deal precisely with this kind of trauma."

He should know.

"When I first moved here there was counselling." She rattled off a few truisms from those early days. "There wasn't anything I could do. I would've been killed, too. Look at all of the good I've done now."

"You *do* know all of those things are true." Finn's eyes were diamond bright with emotion. With compassion. It wasn't pity. And for that she was grateful.

"I do. On an intellectual level." She pressed a hand to her chest. "It's knowing it here that I find just about impossible."

Finn reached across and took Naomi's hands in his own. He looked into her eyes so intensely she was certain he was seeing straight through to the very center of her soul.

"Naomi Collins," he began, his voice gruff with emotion. "There is so much that is wrong with the world. You have seen more of it than anyone should have to. Take it from someone who's seen more than his fair share too. But let me tell you this. The light and the joy that you bring to your patients and to the people who work with you—hell, to anyone who's lucky enough to see that beautiful smile of yours..."

He paused, giving one of her cheeks a soft caress with the back of his hand while rubbing the back of her other hand with the pad of his thumb. Her stomach was doing all sorts of flips and it was just as well Finn opened his mouth to keep on talking, because she was positively tongue-tied with disbelief.

"The light and joy you bring to *me*—and, let me tell you, I'm a pretty grumpy character, so that takes some doing—is more than enough to lighten the burden of any guilt that you bear."

The tangle of emotions that, for so long, had been a tight knot in Naomi's chest felt the first hit of relief. A slackening in the constant tension that she should be doing more, or better.

Telling her story to someone who understood and who didn't judge or blame her for the decisions she'd made all those years ago released something in her she hadn't realized was locked up tight. For the first time in fourteen years she felt it just might be within her power to receive affection.

"Finn?"

He cupped her cheek in one of his broad hands, the edge of his thumb gently stroking along her jawline. "Yes, love?"

"Thank you." And she meant it. With every pore in her body she meant it.

Finn didn't know if it was he or Naomi who had leant into the kiss, but semantics didn't matter at this point. Neither did the fact that finally being able to hold her in his arms was lighting up every part of him like the center of London. One minute they'd been holding hands and the next they'd been kissing and he'd pulled her up and onto his lap. She was straddling him, one hand cupping his face, one hand raking through his hair as if she'd been made to be there. Made to be with him. Gone were all the shy inhibitions he'd thought he'd seen in her earlier.

The same fierce attraction that had pulled them together at the gym was alight. Touch, taste, scent were all threatening to overwhelm him as their kisses moved from tentative and soft to a much deeper exploration of their shared attraction. He wanted this. He wanted *her*. But it had to be right.

What mattered was Naomi and ensuring she wasn't letting the powerhouse of emotions she'd just shared with him lead her into doing anything she would regret.

Using all the willpower he possessed, Finn pulled back from the deep kiss then tipped his forehead to hers, vividly aware of Naomi's soft, sweet breath on his mouth as he spoke. "Are you sure this is what you want? That *I'm* who you want?"

She put her finger on his lips. "Yes."

He captured her hand in his and gave the tips of her fingers a kiss. He wanted this—he wanted her—but not if it was misplaced emotion fueling her desire. "And you'll feel free to stop or tell me if there's any point you don't want to con—"

She dipped her head to kiss him lightly on the lips. "I will." She spoke again, her lips still brushing against his. "There won't be."

She pulled back so he could see her eyes. They shone with certainty. And desire.

Finn's internal temperature ratcheted up a hundred notches as he ran his hands down her sides, enjoying the shift and wriggle of her body's response as he pulled her in close. Two people reveling in the simple pleasure of holding one another. It had been so long since he'd done this and had been emotionally present. She ran her cheek along his stubble then nestled into the nook of his neck for a few slow kisses along his throat.

He heard himself groan with pleasure. And they weren't anywhere near naked yet. As far as he was concerned, they could keep going as slowly and luxuriously as the long winter's night would allow.

"Do you have a bedroom hidden somewhere around here?"

Her smile was one part timid, another part temptress.

"Yes, I do." He rose and took her hand in his,

laying a kiss atop her head as he showed her the way to the bedroom in the stern.

This wasn't pure lust at work. He *cared*. He genuinely cared for this woman and all the beauty and pain she held in that enormous heart of hers.

The night might be a one-off. It could be the start of something more. Either way he would finally know what it was like to be with her after months of wondering. He'd deal with the fallout in the morning.

As she opened the bedroom door and turned to him, eyes filled with questions, he knew that from this moment on, starting with the softest of kisses, the most tender of caresses, he would do everything in his power to make sure she never felt heartache or fear again.

When Finn entered the bedroom, the two of them stood for a moment, frozen between fear and desire. Need trounced tenderness. Hunger savaged restraint. The air crackled with electricity, as if the space between them was a taunt—a dare to see who would be brave enough to make the first move.

Finn's touch was powerful enough to fill the

void Naomi had ached to fill ever since her family had been stolen away from her. As he turned the distance between them to nothing, his scent—a heady wash of pine and man and baking—unleashed a craving in her for more. His caresses, more tender than she had ever known, told her she was no longer alone.

With Finn, she felt invincible. Like a queen who had finally met her true intended after years of isolation and loneliness. With the invincibility also came an unexpected sensation of peace. Cell by cell, her body registered the change.

Their kisses were weighted with intent. With longing. As if they'd known one another far longer than the handful of months Hope Children's Hospital had been open. Their bodies seemed to know one another as if this whole union had simply been a matter of time. Kismet.

She'd never known what it was like to feel whole again.

And when they lay back upon the pillows, a tangle of limbs and duvet and satiation, the tears came. Tears of relief that she still had it in her to love. To believe in a future. Tears of sorrow for the family she would never see again. And through it all Finn held her tight, the beat of his heart keeping time with her own.

A few hours later, Naomi tucked the thick duvet close round Finn's sleeping form, doing her best to work with the gentle sway and rock of the houseboat to quietly tiptoe out of the bedroom, scooping up her discarded pieces of clothing from the floor. Atop a lamp. Hanging from the door handle. Her pants had somehow ended up latched to a hat-rack shaped like a pineapple attached to the wall.

Wow. Finn had some aim.

A slow shimmer of sparkles rippled its way through her bloodstream as she pulled on layer after layer of outdoor clothing in advance of going back to the real world.

Dawn wasn't anywhere near appearing, but already what had happened felt like a moment preserved in aspic. A moment so magical she'd picture it in one of those magic snow globes in her heart because there wasn't any chance something like that could happen again.

Not because she didn't want it to.

In the few hours they had shared in the night

she had felt complete. And it terrified her. It felt like leaving her family behind all over again.

She couldn't burden him with her history. Finn clearly possessed the strength to forge ahead, see the future for what it was—a kaleidoscope of possibility. She wasn't there yet. Not by a long shot. And Finn deserved someone stronger. Someone able to forgive themselves for valuing her own life above others.

She pulled the zip up on her puffer jacket, tugged on her woolly hat and slipped her fingers into her gloves before realizing she was hardly breathing. As if exhaling would make part of the magic of what she'd shared with Finn go away.

She forced herself to breathe out and in again. Reality was only a few short steps away.

She slipped out of his houseboat, crossed the gangplank and urged herself into a gentle run. The cadence of her feet pounding on the footpath drummed in reminders of who she was. Physiotherapist…survivor…

The next word was usually coward. It was her daily process of building herself up only to break herself down again, only this time…this time she kept hearing Finn's soothing words ease away the sharp edges of the accusation she usually hurled at herself.

And yet…trusting that…believing she could still honor the memories of her family and loved ones as well as open her heart to someone and experience such *joy*…it didn't seem possible. It didn't seem *right*.

She pushed herself to run harder, faster. Until she could no longer feel the touch of Finn's fingers on her bare skin. The tickle of the bristles on his chin against her stomach. The warmth of his lips pressing against her own.

Until all she felt was that familiar ache of loss. Only this time it was bigger. This time it wasn't only for what she had lost. But what she would lose if she couldn't release herself from the guilt of having survived what her family had not.

CHAPTER ELEVEN

FINN WOKE UP HAPPY.

Head to toe.

Realizing he was on his own had come as a bit of a shock, but he brushed off Naomi's absence since, for the first time in years, he'd actually slept in. She'd always struck him as an early to bed, early to rise type. Neither did she seem the type to show up in the hospital wearing yesterday's clothes, so…fair enough. Hospital gossip was hard to shake and it had been one night. It was hardly as if they were at the adorable notes on the kitchen table phase of things.

After a brisk shower, he dressed and went back out to the main room, where he stared at the empty kitchen table again. Had he really convinced himself he was cool with the one-night-only thing? Or was this the seismic shift Charlie had warned him would come one day?

Once he'd heard Naomi's story…understood

how deep the waters ran beneath that eternally kind smile of hers...he'd known their paths had crossed for a reason. She was the beacon he'd needed to shine a light on his own life. Show him the bridges he still needed to cross. The truths he needed to confront.

He hit the towpath and walked quickly toward the hospital. An urgent, primal need to see her possessed him. He hunched against the wind and pressed forward. It was cold out. Cold enough to snow if the weather report on his phone was anything to go by.

He followed a group of nurses into the main hospital doors, wondering when he'd last felt this hyped up.

For a surgery?

Months.

Years, maybe.

For a patient?

More recent, but this was different.

For a co-worker he'd just crossed the line from professional to personal with?

Never.

But he'd cross it a million times over if it meant holding Naomi in his arms again.

He knew it as a truth like he knew the thump of his own heartbeat in his chest.

He walked through the hospital's front doors and scanned the huge atrium at the entryway to the hospital. There was no escaping the fact the festive season was creeping up on them fast and furious. Just over two weeks until the big day and the hospital was, courtesy of Evie and her magic elves, reveling in the lead-up.

Two enormous Christmas trees flanked the large glass sliding doors, giving the impression visitors and patients were walking into something more akin to Santa's grotto than a children's hospital, which—he scrubbed at his freshly shaved jaw—he supposed was a good thing.

These poor kids. None of them wanted to be in hospital. Especially at Christmastime. Despite the early hour, he'd bet Naomi was seeking refuge here for exactly the same reasons he'd thrown himself into retraining as a pediatric limb specialist. To forget about herself and pour her energies into her patients.

"Are you planning on making yourself part of the scenery or are you actually going to work?" Marco gave him a jolly thump on the back as he and Alice took off their winter coats and joined him in soaking up the festive atmosphere.

"I don't know. I'd make a pretty cute Santa's helper, don't you think?"

Both Marco and Alice looked slightly surprised to see Finn waggle his eyebrows and do a mini-jig. Well. It was a stationary jig but, hey, he was new at this "jolly chap" thing, so...

"Hey, Finn. While we have you here, you've not got yourself booked up before Christmas, have you?"

He shook his head, though he had a fair few things he knew he'd like to fill his social calendar with and they all sounded a lot like Naomi.

"Go on." Marco gave Alice a loving squeeze. "Show him."

"He doesn't want to see this."

"See what?"

"This." Marco held out Alice's hand just as the sun broke through the clouds. It hit the ring to glittering effect.

Finn pretended to be blinded by the ring's brilliance. "So it's official, then."

"It will be even more so by Christmas. Here..." Marco scribbled a date and a location onto a sticky piece of paper and pressed it on to Finn's chest. "Consider this your early invitation."

Alice laughed and rolled her eyes. "There will be something a bit more official than a sticky note in a few days."

Finn took off the note, put it in his pocket, watching as Alice and Marco wandered off toward the wards, arm in arm. It looked nice. It looked…solid.

"Finn!"

He whirled round and saw a grinning Evie. She was wearing a silly reindeer jumper complete with glowing nose on it.

Why was everyone so *happy* today?

Wait a minute.

He was happy today.

Evie brandished her watch at him. "Countdown to Christmas is officially under way!"

He resisted the curmudgeonly urge to point out that the countdown to Christmas was *always* under way…that was how time worked… and smiled instead.

"Are you still planning on helping out at the Christmas party?" She scanned her clipboard as if suddenly doubting herself. "I've got you down as a yes."

He gave her a distracted yes, not entirely sure if he remembered when the long-awaited party was.

"Bringing anyone?"

That got his attention. There was only one person he'd like as a plus one. Not that he knew where she was. The entire staff of Hope Children's Hospital seemed to be swirling in and out of the atrium, buying coffees, getting first dibs on the fresh-out-of-the-oven mince pies, admiring the decorations. Everything but telling him where Naomi was.

"Finn?" Evie prompted. "Are you bringing anyone tomorrow or are you lending a hand on your own?"

"Why? What's tomorrow?"

Evie gave a faux sigh of exasperation. "What we were just talking about. The Christmas party? For the children?"

"Yes. Right. Of course. No. Maybe." He looked at Evie's list, which appeared to be as long as Santa's list of toys. "Does it matter?"

She gave him a curious glance then shook her head and smiled. "No. Of course it doesn't.

Just as long as we're all there to show the children just how big the Christmas spirit is here at Hope."

"Count me in. You've done an incredible job, Evie. The place is looking magical."

And he meant it, too. The whole world looked different today. Now, if he could only find the person who'd helped change his perspective.

Finn could feel Evie's curious expression on his back as he strode away toward the surgical ward. He had a full roster today and needed to get his head screwed back on straight.

This whole "looking forward" thing was not only messing with his ability to focus, it was adding a bit of a kick to his step.

"Hey, Alana. You and Doodle are looking well today. Hi, Adao."

Naomi waved to Adao from the doorway, waiting for Alana and Doodle to finish their session. Adao's demeanor was still pretty forlorn, even with the curly-haired pooch nestled up beside him on the bed.

Her spirits sagged.

The photo of his parents might've done the trick for a minute or two, but the little boy, now that she had a moment to watch him talk with Doodle, wasn't much chirpier than he'd been that very first day. And who could blame him? He was in pain. He was adjusting to an entirely new way of dealing with his body. The whole hospital was bedecked and beribboned with all the Christmas festivities and he was here all alone.

She knew that feeling so well and yet…for the first time in her adult life she knew she didn't have to. Finn had thrown her a lifeline. A chance to live and see life from an entirely new perspective.

A flight of butterflies took off in her belly as she thought of Finn. His big bear body all tucked in under the duvet looking more peaceful than she'd ever seen him. His arms tightly around her as they'd slept. Well, *he'd* slept, she'd fretted.

The last thing she was going to do was set herself up for more loss.

"I'm afraid it's our time to go, Adao." Alana picked up Doodle's lead and clicked it onto his collar.

Tears welled in the little boy's eyes. "Can't he stay?"

"Not all day, I'm afraid. We've got to go visit some other children and then Doodle's got to go for a walk. Perhaps…" The therapist looked to Naomi for support. "Perhaps when you're feeling a bit stronger, you'll be able to come out for a walk with us."

Naomi smiled. "As long as we get you wrapped up nice and warm, that sounds good to me." She grinned at Adao. "What do you think of that?"

He gave a lackluster shrug.

Poor little guy.

Perhaps going outside was exactly what he needed. Her runs along the river were far more therapeutic than just a bit of physical exercise. Maybe if she could get Adao outside at the party tomorrow…

Alana and Doodle stopped in the doorway so Naomi could give the pooch a cuddle. His furry face was so lovely and open it was little wonder the children felt safe telling him their secrets. She was seriously beginning to think of getting her own dog, seeing how wonderful Doodle was with the children.

Then again… Finn was easy to speak with. And he gave good advice, too, whereas Doodle's talents peaked at furry cuddles. She buried her face in Doodle's curls for a moment, trying to turn her own expression neutral. It was almost impossible to believe the Finn she had just spent the night with was the same man who'd practically bitten her head off every time she'd seen him over the past few months.

To think…all that time it had been attraction holding him at bay.

Mutual attraction.

And it went so much deeper than the physical. Last night she had wanted nothing more than for him to know her. Understand her.

And when she'd taken that risk and told him the raw truth about her past—how shamefully she'd behaved—he'd painted an entirely different picture. He had been so thoughtful. And kind. Not to mention the best kisser she'd met. A ripple of pleasure shimmied down her spine at the memories. Kissing on the sofa. In the kitchen. In his bedroom.

What had possessed her? She'd never behaved like that before with a man. She'd never been so open with *anyone*. Urgh! She wasn't meant to have let herself fall head over heels—

Wait a minute.

Was she in love with Finn?

The thought threatened to overwhelm her so completely she shut it down immediately. Of course she wasn't. She barely knew the man.

Well, that wasn't true. She knew a whole lot more about him now than she had just a handful of days ago. He was generous. A good listener. Amazing with children. Had an ex-wife. Had saved a life. Had an excellent reputation as a surgeon.

What on earth was he doing, wanting someone like her? Someone who'd let her entire family down at the time they'd needed her most?

"Naomi? Is everything all right?"

Alana was peering down at her as she all but kept a stranglehold on the poor therapy dog.

Naomi popped up to standing and gave her leggings an unnecessary swipe. "Yes. Good. Perfect." A crazy laugh burbled up and out of her throat. "Clearly in need of a hug."

"Who needs a hug?"

Her spine slammed ramrod-straight as her heart started jumping up and down as if it had just won the lottery.

Finn.

The man had a way of being there exactly when—when she did and didn't need him.

"No one." She smiled, doing her best to ignore the confusion in his eyes. Steering clear of that intense gaze of his might be the only way she could get through this day. "Adao and I were just going to have a session and Doodle was kind enough to give me a hug on his way out."

"Very generous of the old boy." Finn's tone had slipped from congenial to neutral and, despite the fact Naomi had hoped for things to stay professional, she already missed the warmth in his voice. "Mind if I have a quick word with the lad about his prosthetic casting before you begin?

"Not at all. Adao?"

Adao nodded somberly as Finn talked him through how a team from the prosthetics department would be coming in and taking off his bandages. "But it's nothing to worry about, all right? They're going to cast a mold of your shoulder area and measure your residuum."

"Residuum?" Alana whispered to Naomi.

"It's what's left of his arm. They'll need to measure the shape perfectly so that his prosthesis works well with what he's got left."

"Such a brave little boy." Alana absently

stroked Doodle's head as she spoke, but to Naomi the gesture spoke volumes. She was seeking comfort. Seeing someone you cared about endure pain—no matter how big or small—was hard. Just as her instinct had been to go to Finn when she'd seen him that first time without his prosthesis. Everything in her head had all but screamed out for her to go to him. To help. To help him through his pain.

Now that she actually could go to him—to talk, for a hug, for another one of those spine-tinglingly perfect kisses—acting on it was even more frightening than it had been when he was a virtual stranger.

Because now it mattered if she lost him.

"Right, then. I'll leave you to your session with Naomi, but we'll see you in an hour or so, all right?"

Finn crossed the room to Naomi, who was shifting some paperwork around in a folder. Presumably something to do with her session with Adao.

"Hey." He kept his voice low. "Everything okay?"

"Yes, of course. Why?"

We spent the night together and you disappeared.

"Nothing." They were at work. He wasn't going to press it. "Hey." He gave the door a light pat to get her attention before she began her session. "Do you fancy meeting up for a coffee later or something after work?"

She gave an apologetic shake of the head. "Sorry. Full day today and I promised Evie I'd help get things ready for the party tomorrow." She reached for the door as if to shut it.

"The Christmas party?" He held it open. She nodded, her eye contact hitting all the points around him but never solidly meeting his gaze.

Had he done anything? Said anything to upset her? If so, he wanted to fix it.

"I've really got to get on." She pressed the door again and this time he dropped his hand and watched it shut. How was that for poetic justice? A door closing right in his face just when he'd thought a new path in life had just opened to him.

Right.

He glanced at his watch. An hour until his next surgery. A poor little girl born with curly toes. Sounded cute. Was actually very painful.

Now that they had exhausted all the physiotherapy routes and waited for her to reach the ripe old age of four to see if her tendons were going to offer her any relief, he was hoping to put an end to that pain today.

He headed to his office, mulling over Naomi's cool reaction to seeing him after last night. He suspected there was a lot more to Naomi's lack of eye contact and polite thanks but, no, thanks to his invitation to meet up than a simple case of "buyer's remorse."

Quite the opposite, he was suspecting.

Intimacy was the one thing he'd been unable to bear when he'd been hurt. A lot of his mates from the military had also struggled to make a start on a relationship—or, even more to the point, hold onto one. Help it flourish and grow.

He grabbed the back of the wheeled chair in his office and let it take his full weight as he picked up his phone from his desk and thumbed through the address book. There was one person who knew exactly what it was like to be an open and loving soul on the receiving end of a person going through hell.

He stared at the phone for a moment then, after years of promising himself he would press "call," he pressed down on the little green receiver icon and lifted the phone to his ear.

Hearing her voice say hello was like being yanked straight back in time—except this time he had perspective. This time he wasn't a raging ball of fury. This time there was gratitude she had been as kind to him as she had.

"Caroline. It's me. Finn."

The line was silent for a moment and he was just about to explain who he was again when she spoke.

"You think I wouldn't recognize your voice after all these years?" There was no acrimony in her voice. No bitterness. He heard children's laughter in the background and a dog bark, followed by Caroline's muffled instructions to take the dog outside while she spoke on the phone. An old friend was on the line.

An old friend.

Generous of her.

"You've got kids."

"Observant as ever." She laughed easily then gave a little sigh. "I've landed on my feet, Finn. I hope the reason you're calling is to tell me you have, too."

"Tell me about you some more first." He

pushed his chair back from his desk and threw his good leg up onto his desk and gave his knee a rub as she told him how she'd transferred schools after things had fallen apart with him so she could be closer to her family in the Cotswolds. She was a primary school teacher and had stuck with it. After keeping a close guard on her heart for a while, the gentle persistence of a certain black-haired, blue-eyed teacher across the corridor from her classroom had eventually persuaded her she should let herself love again.

They had two children now—Matty and Willow—and a dog named Mutt.

"So-o-o-o...." Caroline persisted. "I'm presuming you're not calling me to tell me bad news or you would've said it by now. Are your parents all right?"

He smiled at the receiver. Even all these years later she still knew him pretty well. As for his news? He was...*by God*...he was pretty sure he was in love again.

"The parents are fine. Tanning like lizards down in Spain." He'd rung them last week and would ring again. Let them know he finally had news on Caroline and that things might have changed for him a bit as well. "I'm sorry," he said.

"For what?" Caroline's hand went back over the receiver as she issued some more instructions to her children, who had burst back indoors again. He heard something about Santa keeping close tabs on them followed by a sudden, obedient silence.

"That usually keeps then in check," Caroline said in such a way he could practically see the smile on her face. She'd always wanted to be a mother and he'd always wanted "just one more tour" before they began a family. Sounds like things had panned out for her just as she'd hoped. Eventually, of course. What was the saying? After the storm came the rainbow. Something like that. Whatever it was, he hoped her rainbow was a double.

"I'm sorry I was such a git," he said. "After... you know...everything."

"You weren't exactly seeing silver linings when you got back, Finn." Caroline's voice was soft. Forgiving. "And it's me who should be thanking you."

"What? For being a right old ass and pushing away the one person who loved me most?"

"Your parents probably had the market on that one." Caroline laughed then fell silent for a moment. "Look, we were kids when we were married. Did I hope and pray it would work out? Of course I did. I loved you."

"Loved?" He knew he was being cheeky, but it was nice to know the vows they'd taken had meant something. They'd meant something to him, and tearing them apart as he had—ruthlessly—had been like destroying part of his own moral code.

"You know what I mean. I'm happy now. Really happy. And I wouldn't be married to this great guy or have these fabulous, extra-noisy kids of mine if things hadn't gone the way they had with us. It took a while, but I see now that I wasn't the person to help you get back up. You were the only one who could do that and you were determined to do it alone."

"That I was." Finn huffed out a laugh. "Turns out it takes a lot longer if you do it on your own."

"Yes, it does." He could picture her nodding and smiling in that endearing way of hers and was heartened to realize the place he had in his heart for Caroline was very firmly in the "cherished friends" section.

"Are you in love, Finn? Is that why you're ringing? I hope to God you're not going to ask my permission, because you've always had my blessing to find joy."

He barked a laugh. "How the hell did you figure that out from a few 'what's been going on for the past twelve years of your life' questions?"

"Ha! I'm *right*. Love that. Totally easy to figure out." He heard her blow on her knuckles and knew she was giving them a bit of a polish on whatever top she was wearing. Most likely a goofy Christmas jumper if she was anything like she used to be.

"Easy how?"

"Easy because you've never rung me before and your voice has a certain puppy-dog quality to it."

"What? Roughty-toughty me? I don't think so."

"I do," Caroline said firmly. "So what's holding you back? You'd better not say it's me, because that ship sailed long ago, my friend." She spoke without animosity and Finn knew she was doing her best to tell him that whatever guilt he had about the past wasn't necessary anymore. She was in a great place and she wouldn't be there if he hadn't left her.

Finn thought for a moment. Losing his leg had ripped him from his past in one cruel instant. He'd never be the lifelong soldier he'd planned on becoming. But it was different for Naomi. She'd not had any sort of closure as far as he could make out. Her internal life still seemed dominated by what she thought she *should* have done. An impossible position to live with when your choices had been life or death.

"I think she might be afraid that if she lets herself love me, she'll lose her link to the past." He didn't tell her Naomi's story. It wasn't his to tell, but it gave Caroline the lie of the land.

"Well, then. I guess someone had better find himself a way to prove to her that it is possible to love again, and still be true to yourself."

"Good advice, Caroline."

"Yeah, well…" She could've said a lot of things here. She'd learned from bitter experience. Life could be cruel when you least expected it. But she didn't. Because she obviously also knew that life could be kind and full of richly rewarding happiness that made near enough anything seem possible. Even convincing the woman he loved that she wasn't betraying her family by opening up her heart again.

"Happy Christmas, Finn," Caroline said.

"Happy Christmas to you, my friend. And thank you."

"Couldn't think of a nicer Christmas present than to hear you've finally found yourself again."

"Took long enough."

"Well, you're tall," she said. Then laughed. They garbled a farewell as her children's quiet time erupted into a spontaneous round of "Jingle Bells."

He said goodbye, not even sure if she heard him, but the warm feeling he had in his chest told him all he needed to know.

Caroline had forgiven him and moved on. All the proof he needed that miracles existed.

Now all he needed to do was show Naomi she could trust him to be there for her. He was ready now. Ready to live his life to the fullest. And the one way it would be the best life possible was to know he would have Naomi by his side.

CHAPTER TWELVE

NAOMI PUSHED HER tray along the counter of the hospital cafeteria, not really seeing the food options. Normally she loved it here. The social atmosphere. Doctors, families, hospital employees all taking a break from "the medicine business" to enjoy a meal. When it wasn't absolutely freezing out, like today, the cafeteria's concertina doors opened up to a small garden that was scattered with picnic tables.

"Do you mind if I take that?"

Naomi turned to see Madison Archer, the diagnostician from America, reaching for the last bowl of Christmas pudding drowning in a puddle of custard. Truly healthy fare for a hospital.

Her shoulders hunched up around her ears as she inhaled and let out a sigh. It was Christmas. People deserved a treat.

"It's all yours," she said to Madison, even though it was a bit of a moot point at this juncture. "Enjoy." She tacked that on to make herself sound cheerier than she felt.

"Is that what you're eating?" Madison asked as they shuffled up the queue a couple more steps.

Naomi stared at her tray as if seeing it for the first time. A bowl of applesauce. A plate of spaghetti. And a yoghurt.

"Nothing on there really looks like it matches." Madison reached across Naomi toward the fruit bowl and pointed at a banana just out of reach. Naomi handed it to her. "So. Are you pregnant?"

Naomi's eyes went wide. She and Finn had used protection and it wasn't like she wanted children right away anyhow— Wait. No. This whole line of thought was completely going in the wrong direction.

Madison unleashed a triumphant smile. "Am I right?" She gave a little air punch. "God, I needed a win."

Naomi winced an apology. "Sorry. I'm just distracted. Not pregnant." She stared at her tray of mismatched food and bought it all anyhow. She could put the yoghurt in the staff fridge for later when she was filling up gift bags for the children…also known as avoiding Finn so he could forget about her as soon as possible.

She gave Madison a quick smile then wound her way through the lunchtime crowd to the one free table in the room.

A bite or two into her spaghetti she laid down her fork. Nothing was right today. Ever since she'd left Finn's houseboat without leaving so much as a note, the entire day had felt off kilter.

"Sorry. All the other tables are full and I've not really found an office to claim as my own yet. Do you mind?" Madison was already settling down in the chair, so Naomi scooched her tray over a bit to make room for her. More quizzes on whether or not she was pregnant were definitely not what she was after. She would've eaten in the gym, but every time she'd walked in there today all she'd been able to think of was Finn…a shirtless Finn…and being kissed by him and held by him and— *Urgh.*

Stop. Thinking. About. Finn.

"Enjoying your stay?" Naomi asked, to cover the fact that she was playing with her food and the few bites she had taken had tasted like cardboard.

"Not particularly," said Madison, stabbing at one of the small roast potatoes that had come with her chicken and vegetables.

Naomi sat back in her chair and looked at the forthright woman across from her, then laughed. "You've definitely not let the English way of covering up how you really feel get to you, then."

Madison shrugged. "Why would I do that? Wastes time. And energy." She cut off a piece of chicken and brandished it in Naomi's face. "If I could just get disease to be as forthright as I am, I would be one happy customer." She ate her chicken.

"If only life could be that simple."

"But it isn't, is it?" Madison pounced on the statement. "It's a complex, difficult and solitary business." The diagnostician didn't seem angry about it. That was just the way life was. She stabbed another potato with her fork and popped it into her mouth.

Naomi was about to protest when she realized she had actually been living her own life precisely as Madison had succinctly put it. Definitely the solitary part. But who at the end of the day was she protecting? Certainly not her family. Whether she was happy or sad, single or falling in love, it would never change what had happened to them.

"Do you think it has to be? Solitary?"

Madison's green eyes widened at the question then softened. "Maybe not. I just find it's easiest." She stared at her plate for a moment then stood. "I think I'll finish this pudding thing on the ward. See if the ensuing sugar high gives me any insight."

"Ivy?" Naomi asked.

"Hmm." Madison scanned the room as if looking for an escape route.

"The trays go over there. Against the wall." Naomi rose with her own tray. She didn't have much of an appetite either.

"Too many mince pies?" Madison asked, as her final stab at conversation.

"Something like that," Naomi said to Madison's back as the redhead slid her tray onto the rack and headed toward the cafeteria's main doors where an all-too-familiar figure appeared.

"Butterflies, more like," Naomi whispered, as she turned and headed for a side exit. "Definitely butterflies."

* * *

Finn glanced through the glass doors into the gym and saw Naomi putting away some equipment from a session with a patient. A pretty strong one, from the looks of the weights she was hoiking about. Now that he was finally being honest with himself, admitting that he loved Naomi, it was a true pleasure to watch her pootle about the gym, slipping things into place, having little conversations with herself—presumably about one patient or another.

When she looked up, those warm eyes of hers lit up when she saw him, and just as quickly dulled.

He pushed through the swinging gym doors. No point in standing outside like a creepy stalker. Besides, he had to get down to the sports center.

"Hey, there."

"Hi." Naomi started rearranging the weights he'd only just seen her settle into place. Unnecessary busy work.

"I'm just going to put it out there. It seems like you're avoiding me."

A nervous laugh formed a protective bubble

around Naomi, telling him all he needed to know. "No. Of course not."

"So…" He sat down on one of the large balancing balls in the room and stared at his hands for a moment. "Why am I getting the opposite impression?"

"I'm not avoiding you," she said, dodging meeting the clear gray of his eyes as she spoke. "I just… It's been busy."

"Too busy to come out for a mug of hot chocolate?" He pointed in the direction of the atrium. "My shout."

"No. Sorry. I…"

Finn watched as she floundered for an excuse and decided to put her out of her misery. He rose from the balancing ball and cupped her shoulders in his hands. "I liked what happened between us the other night. Did it scare the hell out of me? Absolutely. Do I want it to happen again? Definitely. Will I encounter some stumbling blocks in unveiling the true Charm Machine that lives somewhere under this grumpy bear exterior? I hope so. For you. For me. For what I think could be an 'us'… I really hope so."

Naomi wriggled out from beneath his hands.

"Thank you. I've just— I've got a lot to do tonight."

"This wouldn't have anything to do with feeling guilty about letting yourself actually enjoy your life, would it?"

From the sharp look of dismay that creased her features Finn knew he'd hit the nail on the head.

"Hey." He brushed the back of his hand along her soft cheek. "I know what you're feeling. And if you believe you can trust in that, trust in me. I will be here for you when you're ready."

An hour later, down at the sports center, the feeling that he might've pushed too hard kept losing Finn point after point.

"I hope she's worth it," Charlie called out as he threw the basketball through the hoop with a fluid swoosh.

"Who?"

Playing dumb had been one of his fortes during the dark years. But it didn't always work with Charlie.

"The woman giving you a taste of your own medicine."

"And what medicine is that exactly?" Finn grunted as Charlie threw the ball at him. Hard.

"The kind of medicine a man deserves when he's pushed and pushed every woman who's ever tried to get close to him as far away as he can and then, when he falls hook, line and sinker, is made to work for it."

"That obvious?"

"That obvious."

Charlie wheeled to the side of the court and chalked up his hands then came back to give Finn a quick once-over. "You've got The Look."

"The Look? What the hell is that?"

"All doe-eyed and soppy-faced—"

Finn punched him in the arm. "There isn't a doe-eyed cell in my body."

"Rubbish. You're one of the most romantic men I've ever met. It's why you fell to bits after..." Charlie tipped his head toward Finn's leg, his expression as sober as a judge's. "You wanted things to be perfect. Your vision for how you saw your life, army, marriage, the whole shebang had been all planned out. You hadn't planned on this happening. Not ever again. Well, my friend, it's happened. So how are you going to deal with it? Fight or flight?"

Despite himself, Finn laughed. There was no point in acting the fool in front of Charlie. He dropped onto the bench next to where Charlie had wheeled his chair. "All right, then, O Wise One. What do you prescribe to make sure I don't follow old patterns?"

Charlie leaned back in his chair and stroked an invisible beard. "Listen, my son, to the wise man who has been married many years. To win this woman's heart, you must be there."

"Be there?" Finn had been prepared for a half-hour lecture on understanding the finer points of a woman's psychology, but this was clearly all he was getting.

"That's the one." Charlie nodded, the idea of a beard clearly growing on him as he continued to "stroke" it, waiting for the light bulb to ping on with Finn.

Finn scrubbed a towel over his head and draped it across his shoulders.

Be there.

Charlie was right. Naomi had not only lost her family and boyfriend that day. She'd lost her home town. Her country. Her birthright.

No wonder it was hard to commit to him. Falling in love with someone so different, so far away from the life…the light bulb went on…*the life she'd thought she'd have.* To fall in love with him, Naomi would have to let go of every single childhood hope and dream and allow herself to believe in a new Naomi. A new life. A new set of dreams. All at the expense of everything she'd ever believed would be true.

He snapped Charlie with his towel. "Who made you so wise?"

Charlie gave his invisible beard a final stroke then grinned. "A really good friend saved my life once. Puts a lot of things into perspective." He popped a wheelie in his chair. "That. And I married a woman who told me if I so much as thought of checking out on her when the going got tough I was going to wish I was dead once she'd got through with me!"

They laughed.

"You got a good one," Finn said.

"And so is Naomi. I could tell that the moment I set eyes on her."

Finn gave him a how-the-hell-did-you-know-it-was-Naomi? glare and Charlie guffawed. "Mate. Your face was puppy dog from the moment she entered this sports center. You are a goner." He wheeled around him and pointed at him. "But not in the real sense. Remember. Be there. That's the most important thing."

CHAPTER THIRTEEN

DESPITE ALL THE confusion knocking around her head about Finn, Naomi couldn't help but feel a growing fizz of excitement over the Christmas party at the hospital today.

Evie had seriously outdone herself. She had stayed with Naomi for two extra hours at the hospital last night to sort out some of the final decorations. Naomi had watched, transfixed, as she'd handed over her precious little one, Grace, to Ryan with a thousand words of warning on how to care for her. He'd laughed and kissed her, reminding his future bride he was a doctor and, as a pediatric heart surgeon, had a rough idea how to care for infants.

Naomi pulled on the silly Christmas jumper Evie had given her last night in thanks for helping. When she pulled on the ivory top, edged round the sleeves, hem and neckline with holly-berry-red stitching, she had to admit, she'd drawn the lucky card.

Where other doctors were being doled out jumpers complete with blinking lights or designs that made them look like miniature elves or pot-bellied Santas, hers was almost elegant. A pair of gold antlers was stitched into the fabric and "floated' above a perfect red nose.

She considered her reflection in the mirror, twisting this way and that, only stopping when she realized she was being this vain because she was wondering what Finn would think.

Her heart was already telling her. Finn was looking to the future…a future with her…if only she would take his hand and join him.

Had he spelled it out? No. Had she seen it in his eyes each time she'd dodged his attempts to talk? Without a doubt.

This was up to her now. She looked into the mirror again. Without having even noticed, she'd woven her hands together in front of her heart as if they were providing some sort of shield. But what was it she really wanted protection from? Happiness?

It seemed ridiculous and yet… Allowing herself the true happiness of falling in love and all that could follow in true love's wake, was that bigger than living with the constant fear that she'd never be entirely present? That part of her would always be in Africa?

Her phone buzzed on the little table by her front door.

Evie. She was already down at the hospital, wondering if Naomi fancied coming along to help get the ball rolling.

A few hours later and Evie finally admitted there was nothing left to be done, apart from have the actual party.

The small green in front of the hospital had been utterly transformed from a frost-covered, plain expanse of grass to a winter wonderland.

"All we need is snow," Naomi sighed.

"That," agreed Evie," would be the icing on the cake."

Together the pair of them looked up at the sky then took in the party scene spread out before them. A bouncy castle shaped like an ice palace was nestled in amongst about a dozen stalls all giving away warm, spiced apple juice or hot chocolate. Others had platters filled with amazing glittery cake pops shaped like miniature Santas and snowmen. There were star-shaped cheese crackers and even a huge Christmas-tree-shaped vegetable platter with a pretzel "trunk" surrounded by all sorts of tasty-looking dips. An enormous tray of reindeer-shaped sandwiches was already doing the rounds with curly pretzels standing in as antlers and a perfect roundel of red radish taking the role of the nose. At the far end of the smattering of stalls hosting games for the children was a carousel! Where on earth Evie had magicked that up remained a mystery. Whenever Naomi asked, Evie would just tap the side of her nose and say, "I've got love on my side. Anything's possible when you're in love."

Anything except changing the past.

It felt discordant to have such a gloomy thought when everything about her was all sparkles and glitter and twinkling magic. Maybe a bit of Evie's "love magic" would rub off on her.

Only if you let it, you numpty.

And she wasn't ready to let go. Not yet. Maybe not ever.

"Want a gingerbread man?" Evie held out a cheerily decorated biscuit to Naomi, dancing it toward her with a zany jigging movement. She looked every bit as excited as the children who were starting to arrive from the main entrance of the hospital, all bundled up in their warmest winter clothing, with nurses, parents and scores of others.

Naomi laughed and took the biscuit, holding it slightly aloft as Evie shot past her to attend to a red baubles or silver baubles crisis while Naomi went through the age-old conundrum of deciding whether to bite the gingerbread man's head off or start with his foot.

"I bet you go with the foot first. Then he'll look like me."

Finn's deep voice crackled like a warm hit of electricity along her spine and, despite the urge to run away, Naomi forced herself to turn around and smile. She couldn't imagine him making a joke about his leg a few weeks ago.

A few weeks ago she hadn't been able to imagine him being *nice* to her, let alone setting her entire body alight with a single brush of his hand. The least she could do was afford him a festive smile. She made a show of biting the hand off, knowing it was a contrary move, but he was disarming her. His gray eyes seemed to hold an extra luster today, jewel-bright against the dark clouds gathering in the distance. He was wearing a scarlet-colored hat that made the dark curls peeking through seem even more mahogany rich than they did without it.

He had what looked like a hand-knitted scarf, dark blue, wrapped round his neck and was wearing a light blue jumper with…gold antlers and a single red nose.

"We match." Finn stretched out his jumper as proof.

Oh, yes, they did. In so many ways.

A warmth lit up her belly as her body took its time remembering just how much they did match.

Unable to hold his gaze, her eyes flicked away from his, scanning the large green, hoping an excuse to run away would jump out at her.

"This is all looking pretty spectacular."

Finn reached out and put his hand on the small of her back as a woman led an immaculately groomed Shetland pony past them and toward a small trap that had been reconfigured to look like a sleigh.

A part of her was desperate to bolt and seek refuge somewhere quiet and solitary, while another part of her wanted to feel that lovely, large hand of his touch her back until the end of time. Despite the layers of fabric between them, heat radiated from the spot where he held his hand and it took all the power she possessed not to lean into it. Heck. It took all the power she possessed not to go up on tiptoe and throw her arms around him and tell him she knew she was being strange, but she was scared and her fear was her problem and hers alone.

"Naomi." Finn shifted round so he was facing her. "I know things have been a bit awkward between us since..." His eyes flicked down toward the river with enough meaning in them to indicate the night they'd spent in his houseboat. "What do you say we start again with a clean slate?" He performed a courtly bow. "Would you do me the honor of coming to this afternoon's party with me as my date?"

Her heart skipped a beat at the invitation. The warmth in his eyes told her so much. He was willing to take it slowly. Go at her pace. *Be there for her.* That someone could be so kind, so generous threatened to change the cadence of her racing heart. It was a risk she simply found too terrifying. Patients came and went. That she could cope with. But loving and losing again?

Is it worth losing him without having even let yourself try loving him?

The ache in her heart threatened to tear her in two. She simply didn't know and choosing to be alone seemed the safest option. Always had been. Always would.

"I've got to go and get Adao," she finally said apologetically, when the intensity of Finn's gaze became too much. "I promised him I'd be his date."

A flash of something all too easy to read shot across Finn's eyes.

Hurt.

It twisted her heart so tightly she could barely breathe. "Excuse me." She gave his arm a quick squeeze then set off at a jog toward the hospital entrance, weaving in and out of the crowds of children, their parents, their doctors and nurses, all wreathed in smiles and bathed in laughter as they saw the magical world Evie had created for them.

Questions assaulted her with each step she took.

Why couldn't she let that joy into her own heart?

Why couldn't she allow Finn to shine some light into her world after such a very long time of living cloaked under the weight of guilt and sorrow?

Because they were your family *and you left them behind.*

"Oops. You going in or coming out?" Alice Baxter was wheeling a child out of the front door.

"In. To get a patient," she hastily explained, stepping out of the heavy flow of traffic heading out to the green. From where she was standing, there was already a queue forming at Santa's grotto.

"Have you seen Marco?"

Naomi smiled. She knew Marco Ricci was the one who had put that non-stop smile onto Alice's face.

"I'm pretty sure I saw him with a set of

twins. Twelve-year-old boys, both of them on crutches."

A slip and fall on the ice hockey rink in a spat over a home goal, if she remembered correctly. They were both scheduled to come in to have some physio when their casts came off.

"Excellent. See you out there!" She dropped Naomi a quick wink as she passed. "With any luck, I'll find Marco under the mistletoe!"

Wow. Everyone seemed to have sunbeams shooting out of their ears today.

Little wonder.

Alice was in love.

Evie was in love.

Obviously the same was true for Marco and Ryan.

It was as if the mistletoe fairy had come and sprinkled her fairy love dust over the whole of Hope Children's Hospital...

Was there anyone in this place who wasn't in love besides...?

Her shoulders drooped as her spirits plummeted to the bottom of her boots. *You could be too if you let yourself.*

She gave herself a quick shake and slipped through the traffic coming out the main door.

Adao.

She needed to get Adao and spend the day with him. That would keep her nice and distracted. No more thoughts about love or tall, gorgeous, ex-servicemen turned surgical geniuses needed here. Especially not ones with hands that drove her body wild when—

Naomi pressed her lips together hard and jabbed the elevator button so hard it hurt.

Served her right.

For everything.

Her focus should be on Adao. And after that there'd be another patient and another and another until... How long would she have to keep paying penance for something she couldn't have changed?

Fourteen more years?

Never?

Forgiveness came in many forms. She'd said that once to a parent chastising themselves for taking their eye off their child who had fallen and broken their arm.

Forgiveness comes in many forms.

The question was, would she ever be ready

to forgive herself? Until that happened, she would always be alone.

Finn lifted the three-year-old off the carousel and gently deposited her in her mother's arms.

"Have a lovely afternoon."

What the hell? He sounded like one of his mum's friends after they'd popped round for tea.

"Thanks so much." The mum smiled and whirled around, both her and her daughter's cheeks pink with a combination of the fresh winter air and the exhilaration of the afternoon. If they were giving out medals today, Evie deserved a gold. No doubt about it. The party was a through and through success.

"Oops. Easy there, Adao."

Finn whirled round at the sound of Naomi and Adao's voices.

"Need a hand getting onto the carousel?"

Naomi's dark eyes flicked up to meet Finn's. He hated seeing the panic in them when she saw it was him.

"Yes, please, Mr. Morgan," Adao piped up. "May I ride the black one?"

Finn smiled down at Adao. It was nice to

see the little guy up and about. Apart from the rumored smile when he'd received the picture of his parents, he remained as somber as ever. His arm was healing nicely and within a few days he should be fitted for the prosthetic that was being made at a special factory that supplied them.

"Absolutely. We just need to let it come to a stop so we can get you safely up there and then you can have a ride. Sound good?"

Adao nodded as if he had just agreed to accept responsibility for Finn's most prized horse.

Finn enjoyed watching Naomi interact with the little boy. Kneeling down when she spoke to him so they were eye to eye. Assuring him that "proper riders" only used one hand for the reins.

When the carousel came to a halt again, Finn helped Adao up and onto a glistening ebony stallion, avoiding jogging his arm as much as he could. The stallion's mane was painted a shimmering gold with a saddle painted on in shades of deep reds and oranges.

Naomi walked round to the far side to help offer Adao support if he needed it, but for now he was holding on tight to the stallion's reins, his face serious as the carousel began to turn and the horse began to "gallop" up and down.

Still avoiding eye contact with Finn, Naomi began to jog in place, pretending to try and keep up with Adao as his horse "galloped' forward.

"I'm just about there! I'm coming to get you."

The corners of Adao's mouth began to twitch as Naomi carried on with her jape, dropping her hands to her knees to pant for a moment then straining to "catch up" as the horse leapt and dipped with the rhythm of the festive music.

Finn watched, delighted, as, at long last, Adao's face lit up with a genuine smile. His smile spread like sunshine and lit up Naomi's features as well. He knew it had only been a few days since he'd seen her share a genuine laugh with someone, but it felt like it had been weeks.

Naomi leant in to ask Adao a question.

He didn't quite catch what she'd said, but the words "Christmas" and "wish" leapt out at him.

He could've told Naomi in a second what his was. But this was Adao's time so he watched as the young boy's expression grew very still as he considered his options.

The music began to slow, along with the movement of the carousel, just as Adao seemed to make up his mind.

"For Christmas," he began, "I would love to see my parents. And I would love to see snow."

Tears sprung instantly to Naomi's eyes when Adao mentioned his parents. It was a wish neither of them could grant. And no doubt was doubly painful for Naomi to hear, knowing she would most likely never know what had happened to her own family.

As for the snow… He looked over his shoulder at the gray clouds moving in from across the fens. He looked straight up to heaven and threw in a silent request that at least one of the boy's two wishes could come true. As for Naomi…he needed her to know the truth about him. See how far he'd come before she completely wrote him off. He was living proof that life was full of second chances.

"Let's get you off there, mate." Finn lifted Adao up and off the horse, noting how light he was, and how receptively he responded when Finn pulled him in close for a bit of a hug before he put him down.

Evie rushed up all smiles and twinkling eyes.

"Adao! Just the man I was looking for. Do you think you'd like to come along and meet Father Christmas?" She shot a quick look at Finn and Naomi. "Would it be all right if I steal him for half an hour? We could meet at, say…how about at the Pin the Tail on the Reindeer stand at half-past?"

"Absolutely." Naomi's voice was bright, though Finn sensed a note of reluctance to let the little boy out of her sight.

"How 'bout I take care of this one?" Finn pointed to Naomi. "And you take care of this one." He pulled his own knitted cap off his head and tugged it onto Adao's. "And we'll meet up for apple cider doughnuts and a warm drink after."

"Sounds great." Evie grinned at the pair of them then stuck out a mittened hand to Adao. "Ready to meet the big guy?"

Adao's eyes shone with delight as he slipped his hand into Evie's.

"Right!" Finn clapped his hands together and gave them a brisk rub before putting them gently on Naomi's shoulders. "You and me. We need to talk."

CHAPTER FOURTEEN

NAOMI TRIED HER best to look relaxed as she and Finn strolled away from the party and down toward the river.

"From the look on your face people are going to think I'm kidnapping you!" Finn gave her a playful nudge with his elbow and tried to rouse a smile.

He wasn't successful.

She felt nervous and as if her heart was being yanked from one side of her chest to the other.

Sure. The angst was all of her own making, but…why couldn't Finn just let sleeping dogs lie?

"It's so cold I think we'd better forgo the bench and just keep on walking, if that's all right."

"Of course." She glanced back at the party scene behind them.

"Don't worry, love." He wrapped an arm around her shoulders and gave her a light squeeze. "I'll get you back to Adao." He dropped his arm from round her shoulders and instantly she felt the loss of contact.

"I want to tell you a bit more about me after my accident."

"You don't have to," Naomi quickly jumped in. She knew how painful trips down memory lane were and yet…she'd wanted him to know about her past. "I'm sorry. Please. Go ahead."

Finn gave her a thin smile of thanks, clearly already halfway back on his journey to the past. "After I lost my leg I was in a rage with the world. As you know, I was married at the time and the truth of the matter was I didn't handle it well. Not at all. From a young age I had everything all planned out. I would be in the army like my dad. I would teach my kid brother to do the same so I could look after him—"

"You have a little brother?"

Finn's smile was tight and his eyes didn't meet hers, so she knew the memories were painful. "I do. And there are still some fences that need mending on that front. He's a career military man. Always traveling. Mostly peace-keeping tours, but…he's out there, doing the family thing."

Naomi shook her head. "What do you mean?"

"Morgans have always been military. As far back as we can trace. When I became the first one to drop the baton—"

"You didn't 'drop the baton'!" Naomi was indignant. He'd sacrificed himself to save a fellow soldier. A friend. A life.

Finn took her hand in his and gave it a squeeze. For the first time in days it felt right and she gave his fingers a squeeze back so he would know she was there, listening.

"It felt like it. I thought I'd let my family down. And my wife. It wasn't the future I had promised her. Wasn't the future I had promised myself, and the only way I thought I could deal with it was on my own so I pushed and pushed until there wasn't anyone around me anymore and I'd got exactly what I'd wished for."

"And?" Naomi knew there was a big "but" lingering out there and felt a twitch of nerves, wondering what it was.

"But…" Finn grinned at her as if he'd been reading her thoughts. "Being alone, going through what I'd been through on my own was about the dumbest thing I think I'd ever done."

"So...do you regret getting divorced?"

"Yes. No." He quickly shifted course. "Our vows meant a lot to me. To both of us. And not coming good on them was a lot to face up to. So, for a long time, I didn't. Just pushed her and everyone else who mattered away." He looked up to the sky for a minute before continuing. "Caroline's in a great place now, and to be honest? I don't know that she and I would be a match...the people we are now. We were married very young and neither of us was ready to take on the challenges that my injury brought along with it. The minute I'd decided to retrain as a pediatric surgeon, that was all I had room for in my life. I simply shut her and anyone else who cared right out of the picture."

"What about Charlie?" Naomi was completely lost in Finn's story now. She knew exactly what he meant. The same drive he'd used to retrain as a surgeon sounded so similar to how she'd poured herself into her physiotherapy studies. Like it had been a mission. And yet...she had a feeling Finn's tale came with a lesson. One she might benefit from learning herself.

"Charlie?" Finn laughed. "Charlie was the one who knocked me on the head and demanded I start being more sociable. As far as I was concerned, doing surgeries and skulking round my houseboat were good enough for me. But when he introduced me to those kids and the lads on the wheelchair team, I slowly began to see what an idiot I'd been. But I was still compartmentalizing."

"Until…?" There had to be an "until" because Finn was completely different from the gruff, standoffish man she'd met at that first staff meeting.

He turned and faced her, eyes alight with emotion. "Until I met you."

"Me?"

"Yes," he said softly, stroking her cheek with the back of his hand. "You. You made me want to live again."

"What are you talking about? You're the one who went to the sports center. You…you… made marshmallows!"

"That wasn't living, love. That was going through the motions. Charlie used to harangue me like an old harpy. 'Come down to the gym! Do this! Do that! If you don't come for tea the trouble and strife'll have my head!'"

Naomi laughed at his spot-on imitation of Charlie, then looked up to the sky, trying to collect her thoughts. "Why are you telling me all this?"

"I think you know damn well why I'm telling you," Finn said gently. "I'm in love with you and I think you feel the same way, but you're scared."

Tears sprang to her eyes and she was half-tempted to ask if he'd also been retraining as a psychic. "How do you know?"

"Because I know what it feels like to carry a burden of guilt around. I know how terrifying it feels to let yourself be happy when you hold yourself responsible for causing the ones you loved so much pain."

He took her hands in his and dropped kisses on her knuckles. "Naomi, what happened to your family is not your burden to carry. What you can and should carry in your heart are all the happy memories. The joy."

Tears began to trickle down her cheeks. Finn tugged a handkerchief out of his winter coat pocket and held it out to her. "I brought extras just in case."

She giggled through her tears, despite herself. "You came prepared?"

"I try to always come prepared." He gave her a cheeky grin.

"Army boy," they said in tandem then stopped, frozen in each other's gazes as if they'd been given a heaven-sent reminder that they were and should be together.

"You're right, you know," Naomi finally admitted.

"About what?"

"All of it. The guilt. Not wanting to let go. Not wanting to let myself admit that…" A hint of shyness overcame her. Finn, once again, seemed to read her mind and dropped a kiss on her forehead.

"It would be the first time in a long time anyone admitted I was worth loving."

"I want to be that person." Naomi spoke in a rush, acutely aware that if she let this pass with Finn—this love that really could grow into something wonderful—she would be letting an enormous part of what it meant to be alive pass her by. Because what was the point if there wasn't love?

"I love them so very much," she admitted. "But I can't do anything to change what's happened."

Finn nodded along as she spoke. "It's the double-edged sword of loving. Loving and losing," he clarified. "Look, I was determined to spend the rest of my days on my own. I didn't want to hurt anyone the way I'd hurt Caroline ever again, but you know what? I rang her the other day and wouldn't you know it? She's as happy as Larry."

"Who's Larry? How do you know that he's happy?"

Finn threw his head back and laughed a full-bodied laugh. A warmth grew in her chest, a happiness that she'd been the one to set him off.

He pulled her close to him, so close she could feel his heartbeat through his winter coat. "Larry is a very happy guy," Finn said. "And I will be too if you'd agree to give this thing a shot with me. I want to live again, Naomi. I want to love and laugh and..." his voice went all rumbly "...make love. And I'd like you to be the woman I do all those things with." He held her out at arm's length. "You deserve happiness, Naomi. You deserve to live a full, rich, incredible life. What do you say? You and me doing our best to make our peace with the past and give ourselves a shot at a happy future?"

She stared up into Finn's gray eyes and knew she could look into them forever. He truly understood her. Her fears, the terrifying experiences she'd been through. Her reluctance to let herself experience unfettered happiness. And yet...he was willing to try it. And when she was with him, she felt brave, too. She'd already had a glimpse into the joy of being with someone who made her insides fluttery and her heart skippity. She already knew she was in love. It was simply a question of saying... "Yes."

Finn stared at her as if in shock. "Yes?"

Her grin widened along with his. "Yes!" She shouted it out and a pair of swans took flight from the river.

"Well, then, my little flower blossom..." Finn pulled her close to him and cupped her face in his big hands "...I think we'd best seal this deal with a kiss."

"You think?" Naomi teased.

"I know," Finn growled, kissing her with a sensual confidence that came with truth and honesty and love.

"He's over here!" Finn hadn't felt this happy in he didn't know how long. A beautiful woman by his side, a chance to look forward rather than dwelling on the past and, best yet, snow!

"Adao!" Naomi waved her arms when the boy turned to them, a cup of steaming hot chocolate in his hands.

"Finn! Naomi!" Evie waved them over. "I jumped the gun when the snow began and ordered some hot chocolate. You in?"

"Of course." Finn looked up at the sky, enjoying the sensation of the big, fat flakes falling on his face, then knelt down so he was eye to eye with Adao. "What do you think, little man? Does it live up to its reputation?"

"Even better."

Naomi laughed and gave the knitted cap on his head a bit of a tweak. "Looks like it's definitely a day for Christmas wishes to come true."

She laughed, enjoying the comforting sensation of Finn nestling in close to her, then leaning in even closer so that he could whisper into her ear.

"Was I *your* Christmas wish?"

"Something like that."

He feigned looking affronted. "Just something?"

"Exactly." She gave his hand a squeeze, already excited for the next time they could be alone and share more of those luxurious, life-affirming kisses. "Exactly what I wished for."

And he was. Finn had helped her see the only person she was hurting was herself. She scanned the party area as she sipped her hot chocolate and listened to Adao tell Finn all about his time with Father Christmas. The only thing she needed to do now was find a little sprig of mistletoe and then all her Christmas wishes would come true.

CHAPTER FIFTEEN

A year later

"MUM… BAABA…" ADAO beamed at his mother and father as they stepped into the hospital's foyer, which was decked out with two huge trees the hospital had decorated in their usual incredible fun-loving style. "This is Naomi. And this is Mr. Morgan."

"Finn," Finn corrected, as he stepped forward to shake hands with the couple who had just been flown in. "Lovely to meet you, Mr. and Mrs. Weza. And you must be…"

"Imani." Adao's sister didn't suffer from shyness in the slightest. She shook hands with Naomi and Finn and beamed. "I can't believe it is snowing!"

"These are just the types of miracles that happen here at Hope Children's Hospital." Naomi shrugged and grinned. The place was magical. Especially under a thick blanket of snow.

"It's amazing to see you here in your working environment," said Mrs. Weza. "After the village, I mean. You seemed so at home there as well."

Finn wrapped his arm around Naomi's shoulders and gave her a kiss on the cheek. "That was an amazing trip. I don't think I've ever had such incredible seafood before."

"It was wonderful of the charity to organize for us to come out and work with Adao. He's progressed so much with his prosthesis. And grown, too!"

Adao beamed. "Nine centimeters in one year!"

"Well above average. In many ways," she added, giving his head a scrub. Seeing his parents again had really brought out the spark in him.

Naomi smiled up at Finn. She couldn't believe how much the pair of them had changed in just a year. Evie had even taken to calling them the Grin Twins.

Well…

When one was in love, why not spread the joy?

The prosthetics specialists spotted them and

joined their group. After a quick discussion about what Adao would have to do to get the mold for his new prosthesis, they suggested his family join him so they could all see.

"It was really lovely meeting you."

"We'll see you again before we go, right?" Adao threw his arms round Naomi's waist and gave her a huge hug. His new prosthesis seemed a part of him now. Proof, as if she needed any, of just how important their work at the hospital and overseas was. She smiled down at him. "Of course we'll see you again. And next year when Finn and I come out again with the charity, we'll see if you can manage to grow as much as you have this year."

"As tall as you!" whooped Adao. "Then the next year as tall as Finn!" The thought struck his entire family as hilariously funny and Naomi felt nothing but warmth and joy in her heart as she watched them laughing their way down the corridor.

"They're a lovely family." Finn slipped his hand round hers and gave it a squeeze.

"That they are."

"Want to go out and have a snowball fight with me?"

Naomi looked at him in disbelief. "I bet you think you'll win."

"I think a lot of things," Finn riposted playfully as he pulled her into a hug.

"You do, don't you?"

"Yes," Finn said airily. "And I'm usually right."

Naomi went up on tiptoe and gave him a quick kiss. "You have been right about a lot of things."

"I know."

He tried to keep a straight face for as long as he could, but Naomi knew the trick to make him break now.

"Tickle fight!"

She ran out the front door, chasing him as he begged her not to tickle him. His weakness, she'd discovered one day when she'd worn nothing but a feather boa to bed.

Finn tripped when he reached the green and Naomi fell on top of him breathless with laughter and joy.

When they had caught their breath, she beamed at him. "I love you, Finn Morgan."

"I love you, too, pretty lady. You make the world—my world—a better place."

"And you helped me see what a lovely place the world is."

They shared a tender kiss before getting up and shaking the snow off themselves. She hoped Finn knew how much she had meant what she'd said. Over the course of the year he had shown such patience and tenderness that sometimes it was hard to believe he was the same man who'd barked at her to leave him alone.

Finn knew her inside and out. Her fears. And now, more importantly, her hopes and dreams.

"Fancy a cup of hot chocolate by the Christmas tree before we get back to work?"

"Absolutely."

Finn reached out his hand and took Naomi's in his. This was the moment he'd been waiting for all year.

Luckily, the hospital "fairies" had waved their magic wands over the green outside the hospital yet again and… Yup! Just over by the enormous candy cane…a mistletoe stand.

"C'mere, you." Finn led her over to the stand.

"What are you up to, you rascal? I thought we were going for hot chocolate."

Finn tipped her chin up and looked straight

into her eyes. "I can do you one better than that, my love."

"Better than hot chocolate on a snowy day?" She laughed. "I don't think so."

He reached into his pocket and pulled out a little light blue box. "How 'bout an early Christmas present?" He flicked open the box and showed her the diamond solitaire he'd been carrying around in his pocket for the last three months.

"A—? What—?"

Finn dropped to one knee, not caring who saw him.

"Naomi Collins Chukwumerije…" He stopped and grinned, clearly pleased with his pronunciation of her surname. "Would you do me the honor of marrying me?"

Her heart stopped for an instant then did a happy dance all its own.

"Oh, Finn… I… Of *course* I'll marry you!"

He leapt to his feet, pulled her into his arms and would've kissed her until the sun went down if some of the other doctors hadn't started wolf-whistling.

"She said yes!"

A huge roar of cheers and applause rose up

around them as he pulled Naomi close to him. "You said yes."

"You're the love of my life," Naomi whispered as he slipped the ring onto her finger. "I can't wait to let the whole rest of the world know."

Together, smiles lighting up their faces, they entered the hospital with their eyes solidly on the future, knowing they had each other to help them in whatever came their way.

* * * * *

LET'S TALK

Romance

For exclusive extracts, competitions
and special offers, find us online:

 facebook.com/millsandboon

 @millsandboonuk

 @millsandboon

Or get in touch on 0844 844 1351*

For all the latest titles coming soon,
visit millsandboon.co.uk/nextmonth

*Calls cost 7p per minute plus your phone company's price per
minute access charge

Want even more
ROMANCE?

Join our bookclub today!

'Mills & Boon books, the perfect way to escape for an hour or so.'

Miss W. Dyer

'Excellent service, promptly delivered and very good subscription choices.'

Miss A. Pearson

'You get fantastic special offers and the chance to get books before they hit the shops'

Mrs V. Hall

Visit millsandbook.co.uk/Bookclub
and save on brand new books.

MILLS & BOON

X017047